The Amish Golden Lights

Hannah Winstone

Published by Trellis Publishing, 2021.

THE AMISH GOLDEN LIGHTS

First edition. July 16, 2021.

ISBN: 979-8224025671

Written by Hannah Winstone.

THE AMISH GOLDEN LIGHTS
HANNAH WINSTONE

The sun shone overhead, casting golden light across the street Beth called home. Across the street her neighbour waved, and Beth waved back as she climbed from her car. Immediately the sun's warmth hit her and she smiled, head tilted to the sky.

She only allowed herself to enjoy it for a moment before going about the task of unloading the shopping. The first one was easy enough; but Beth was a small, thin woman and had a tendency to buy in bulk. The heavier bags refused to budge - and how had she managed to get them in the car in the first place?

"Need help?"

Beth's cheeks flushed at how she jumped, a small squeak passing her lips. When she turned her eyes locked onto a tall, dark-haired man in a button down shirt. "Fine, thanks," she replied with a kind smile, "these are just heavy. Time to hit the gym again, I suppose." Not that Beth ever used the weights when she *did* go.

"I can take these inside for you, it's no trouble." The man's smile was pearly white and so *stunning* for a moment Beth forgot how to breathe. Then he leaned across, his arm barely brushing hers, and scooped up the heaviest shopping bag as if it weighed nothing. "I'm Matthew, by the way. Matthew King."

"Beth Kanagy - uh, Springer." A simple slip up - after using her husband's surname for so many years sometimes she forgot. Forgot she was no longer there, forgot she had her own life now. Memories threatened to swarm her but she shook them away. Instead she focused on the man beside her, still unloading her shopping. "I don't think I've seen you around before?"

"I live in number eighty-five, just moved here a few weeks ago." He beamed at her, and Beth felt her heart jump. "If you open the door, I'll take this inside."

Beth nodded, a smile on her lips - but as she hopped up the steps to her front door, she hesitated. She lived alone save for two cats; and Matthew was a stranger. Letting *any* stranger, never mind a man, into her house gave her pause. But he seemed nice enough so she shook those thoughts away, stuffing them in the back of her mind. She was *fine*. The door slipped open and her ragdoll cat immediately ran to her, mewling like a kitten.

Behind her, Matthew chuckled. "Cute," he laughed, "I've never had a pet. They weren't really a thing where I grew up."

"Me neither," Beth replied, "except for dogs."

"I've always wanted a snake," Matthew replied absently, "something unusual."

They shuffled inside, Matthew disappearing through the kitchen archway to drop the shopping onto the dining table. "Well, that's everything," he called through as Beth kicked off her shoes, "I suppose I should get going."

There was no *reason* for him to stay; yet Beth still found her stomach dropping at the thought. "So soon?" she asked, words slipping from her lips without consent, "would you like to stay for tea? Coffee?"

When Matthew popped his head through the door he positively *beamed*. "Sure, I can stay a while."

So Beth made the coffee; two steaming hot mugs with plenty of cream and a plate of homemade shortbread for them to share. They settled down on the sofa, a respectable distance apart, and Beth found herself more at ease with Matthew than she had ever been with anyone. Even her two cats settled between them, curled up into sleepy little balls. Her cats didn't like *anyone* save for a few close friends.

Beth swirled the coffee in her mug, watching the creamy brown liquid splash against the rim. It felt so *odd* having him in her house, so wrong yet so right. She hadn't had a man in her house since... well, since her husband. But that was two years ago and a hundred miles away.

Matthew said something, voice soft, and Beth blinked. "I'm sorry," she apologised with a soft laugh, "I was lost in thought."

His smile was infectious, and Beth's uneasiness couldn't last. "It's all right," he assured, "I just asked where you were from. Originally, I mean. Your accent isn't local."

"Oh." Beth flushed, sudden embarrassment taking over her thoughts. It wasn't that she was embarrassed about her upbringing, per se, but the baggage that came with it. Hesitantly, she replied, "not far, really. I've never left Tennessee, but my community was pretty secluded. I'm... well, I'm Amish."

She expected questions, either from curiosity or the desire to mock. What she *didn't* expect was for Matthew's eyes to light up and a grin to overtake his handsome features. "Oh, *amazing!* I'm from Iowa, Amish too, but I've lived in Tennessee since I was twenty. I suppose I've lost my accent over the years."

It was true that he had that Tennessee inflection, but not entirely. She smiled, allowing her body to relax. "Imagine us both moving so close to each other," she laughed.

"It sure is a surprise. A good one, though; honestly I don't quite believe it."

Neither did Beth; since moving away from her old life she had ran into perhaps one other person to have left their Amish roots behind. Warmth spread across her face as she smiled, staring into her coffee.

"So, why did you decide to leave? Surely someone as lovely as yourself was popular back home."

The smile vanished. "I..." Beth spluttered, words refusing to pass her lips. "I don't talk about it."

"Oh." It was Matthew's turn to flush, tanned skin turning crimson. "I apologise. It's personal, I shouldn't have asked."

A shrug, noncommittal. "Don't worry about it." She forced a smile, but it fell flat.

He took a moment to stare into his coffee, then set the half finished mug down on the glass coffee table. "I should leave; I'm meeting up with my brother later."

She wanted him to stay - *desperately* - but she saw the awkwardness in the way he shifted his gaze, in the way his hands fumbled with the hem of his shirt. So she relented. "Of course," she replied simply, "thank you for the company, and for helping me with the shopping."

"Any time," he replied kindly - and she knew he meant it.

When she showed him out and watched him saunter down the porch steps, Beth felt her heart soar for reasons she couldn't quite understand.

———————————————

When Beth drew back the curtains the next morning the vibrant sunshine almost blinded her. Blinking, she took a moment to enjoy the warmth streaming through the window.

Then her hazel eyes caught sight of a broad shouldered figure across the road. The light hit the window _just so_ and she couldn't see his face - but her blood ran cold nonetheless. She was being watched. Stalked. A man stood across from her house with his gaze set to her window and she _knew_ what that meant.

Behind her the cats mewled, scratching at the door to be let in. Beth stumbled to the door and flung it open, ignoring the way both cats pawed at her bare legs for attention.

Heart in her throat she returned to the window, afraid of what - _who_ - she might see; but the street was empty. A light flickered on from number seventy-eight across the road, shadows moving behind the curtain. No man stood in the street. There wasn't even a sign of him as Beth cast a wary glance each way.

Was it possible she had imagined it?

Beth's heart rate slowly returned to normal as she dressed. By the time she had brushed her teeth and ran a comb through her messy blonde locks she had rationalised it all away as a mistake made by her sleep addled brain. She tied her hair up in a loose bun at the back of her skull, and she was ready to go about her day.

Yet her mind wouldn't quite allow her to forget the broad shouldered figure.

Downstairs the doorbell rang and Beth let out a squeak - almost tumbling from her bed. She waited with bated breath, not even knowing what to expect - but then she peeked outside and saw a familiar sandy mop of hair. Matthew.

The way she hurried downstairs was perhaps *too* eager, but she couldn't help it. Nor could she help the grin that crossed her face as the door swung wide. "Good morning, Matthew. Is everything okay?"

His smile was bashful, something she hadn't expected to see on such a strong, confident face. His eyes glittered. "Brilliant, actually. I know it's early but I have work this afternoon and... and I wondered if you would like to get breakfast together?"

Beth blinked. Breakfast? With *her?* They had only met one day previously. Her mind went into overdrive, attempting to rationalise his motives. Before she stopped herself she blurted, "are you asking me on a *date?"*

He hesitated to answer - but that in itself told Beth the truth. He shifted, head bowed. "I know we left things awkward between us yesterday, but I like you, Beth. So yes, this *is* a date. If you want it to be."

Small hands clenched around the door handle. She couldn't do this, couldn't go on a *date.* Not after... well, he had no right to know her past. It wasn't something she willingly talked about. "You're lovely, don't get me wrong, but I can't."

He peeked up at her, lips curled. Beth almost *flinched* when he stepped forward, heart shuddering - but he only offered her a gentle hand. "Are you sure? It doesn't have to be a date; it could just be two neighbours getting to know each other."

There was no doubt Beth *wanted to.* Back home she had never dated, not in the modern sense or the Amish sense. Her entire relationship had been arranged from the beginning; from her courting to her marriage. This was *new;* but new wasn't always good.

The silence stretched on, tense and thick and almost *painful.* Matthew stepped down, defeated. "I see," he replied quietly when it became obvious Beth wasn't going to say a thing. "I'm sorry I pushed this on you. I'll back off." When his gaze flickered up, it wasn't difficult to see the hurt in those crystal blue eyes.

A million thoughts whirled through her mind. Apologies. Explanations. Ways to take it back and say *yes, I'd love to go on a date with you.* None of those thoughts passed her lips. They stuck in her throat, choking her.

Matthew hovered by the porch for another moment and at first she thought he had more to say. Then he just sighed, awkwardly backing down in order to turn away.

Overhead the summer sun beamed. It did little to stop the coldness from creeping into Beth's chest.

"I'll uh, see you around?" Matthew muttered with a ghost of a smile.

"Sure," was all Beth thought to say.

Then he disappeared from her porch, feet dragging the ground as if it was physically painful for him to leave. It would have been the perfect time to call out, to apologise, but Beth's lips were tightly shut as she watched him sadly.

By the time he had vanished from her view, Beth was empty. She let the door swing shut, the *thud* shaking the door in its frame. She was alone - and despite having lived alone for two years, this was the emptiest she had ever felt.

———————————————

Instead of going out with friends or catching up on work, Beth spent the weekend replaying her conversations with Matthew over and over in her mind. She came to the conclusion that despite having perfectly valid reasons for acting the way she did, it was unfair. Cruel, even. All he had wanted was to take her out for a meal and she had acted as if it was part of some insidious plan.

So Beth pulled on her coat, grabbed her purse, and headed for number eighty-five. Despite having lived there for two years, Beth didn't know the street all that well; certainly not the winding cul-de-sac the houses eighty through ninety belonged. Eventually she found it; a quaint little brick house with a neatly kept garden and freshly painted front door. There was no car in the drive but a light was on inside; Matthew was home.

Yet still she hesitated to knock. By coming here, was she just making things more awkward? The last thing she wanted was to make a big deal of it, to make Matthew feel even worse. Yet she simply couldn't leave things as they were; not when remember the downward quirk of his lips and the shine in his dark eyes dimming.

Beth raised a small fist to knock - but then she caught a flash of movement from the corner of her eyes and she froze. It could have been a cat, maybe, or a wandering animal from the woods close by. Yet it was too big, too *tall* and humanoid to be an animal. Fear gripped her chest as she forced her head to turn, afraid of what she might see.

The figure was human. Wide shoulders and thick arms hanging by their side. They wore a dark coat that covered their bulk and shrouded their face from view; but it was impossible to mistake that towering frame for anyone else. *Chandler.* Her ex-husband. Ex in mind only; he hadn't allowed them to officially divorce.

Her phone vibrated deep in her pocket and she flinched. Shaking hands fumbled with the device and she nearly dropped it onto the concrete steps. There was a single text, from an unknown number. It was written in full, no text speech save for spelling errors made with clumsy hands. Hands unused to technology.

Come home. Emily misses you.

Innocent enough, but the words made her shiver. When she turned back to the figure, he was gone.

Matthew's front door opened and she sprung back, a shriek parting her lips. The phone tumbled from her hands and she ducked, snatching it up just in time. Chest hammering, she shot her wide gaze upward-

Matthew stood there, eyes wide in surprise. One hand outstretched to help, but then he dropped it to his side. Like he had decided better. "Beth?"

"Uh, hi?" She shoved the phone back in her coat pocket, casting one last wary glance to where Chandler had stood. He was truly gone; for now.

Matthew padded down the steps, brows furrowed in concern. His voice was soft as he asked, "are you okay? Is something wrong?"

Beth hadn't realised she was still shaking until she felt a warm hand against her shoulder. "I... I'm fine," she lied, "I actually came here for you."

"For me?"

There was too much on her mind, too much going on and she couldn't concentrate. Yet when she looked into his dark eyes a sense of calm washed over her, and she smiled. "I want to apologise. The other day when you asked me out, I was horrible. I didn't *mean* to be, but that doesn't make it any better, does it? So I'm sorry."

For a moment he only blinked, taking it all in. Then his full lips curved into a smile and he *laughed.* "It's all right! I understand, really." He hesitated over his next words, but that gorgeous smile never left. "Does this mean you've reconsidered my offer?"

Did it? Beth wasn't sure. She *liked* Matthew, truly - and there wasn't a lot of people nowadays she could say that about. So yes, she wanted to go on a date with him, catch up on all of the things she missed in her old life. Still, she hesitated. Could she really trust again?

"You don't have to," Matthew interrupted her thoughts, "but the offer is still open. I promise I have no hard feelings."

He was nice; too nice really, when she compared him to Chandler. But wasn't that sort of the point? Beth shifted, uncomfortable, and dropped her gaze. "I'd like to," she admitted, "but I have a lot going on right now. I... you know I left my family behind when I left my Amish community?"

"Yes." He smiled, patient and warm, waiting for her to continue.

Beth sucked in a breath. She would tell him only what he *needed* to know; the bare minimum. Even so her stomach rolled and her cheeks burned with shame. "I left behind my husband, too, and he was extremely upset. You understand I *had to,* for my own safety." She ducked her head, cheeks crimson. "I think he knows where I am. I got a text just now - and he doesn't know how to use a phone but who else could it be?"

"Is the threatening you?" Matthew shot up, eyes narrowing and for the first time since she had met him, that softness vanished. "Are you in danger?"

"I... I don't know," she admitted quietly, "but it isn't me I'm worried about."

Matthew paused, lips parted in a silent question.

Beth shifted under the intensity of her gaze and wished the ground could swallow her up. When he didn't say a word, Beth shrank, folding in on herself. "I don't want to talk about it," she muttered, "but I can't go out with you until I know I'm safe. Until I know *she's* safe."

"Call the police," Matthew murmured. Beth parted her lips to reply but then thick arms enveloped her and she was pressed into his chest. His hoodie was soft, warm, and smelled pleasantly of coffee.

Beth inhaled, curling into him without hesitance. How strange that she had meet him only a few days ago and yet *somehow* she trusted him completely. "I'll call them," she murmured against his chest, "but I'm worried it won't help. There's no evidence other than my word. And his."

Matthew pulled her closer, trailing fingers through her thick blonde curls. "Then I'll do what I can to help."

Beth believed him.

———————————

Beth perched on a stool at her breakfast bar with a steaming mug of coffee clasped between her palms. This was the second day in a row she had called in sick and refused to leave the house. That morning she had got out of bed and dressed in her work clothes, only to back down the second she reached for the house keys.

Even her cats knew something was wrong, pawing at her legs and

mewling softly. Someone had told her once that pets were sensitive to that sort of thing. Danger. Emotional distress. *Fear.*

The coffee steam billowed around her as she blew gently, then took a tiny sip. It scalded the tip of her tongue and she winced, setting the mug down.

Her phone buzzed, scooting across the breakfast bar, and Beth flinched. She was almost afraid to look, hands hovering above the screen. She relaxed when it was only a text from her manager, asking when she would be back. *Soon,* she replied, *I'll let you know tomorrow.*

It was obvious that she had to go back eventually. Staying inside, refusing to even step onto the porch for fear of spying Chandler, it wasn't healthy. She had called the police, everything was *fine.* For all she knew she had been arrested already and she would get the call letting her know any minute.

Sure, the doubt in her mind chided, *because it's that easy.*

Her hands clenched around the mug so tightly it *burned,* and she leapt away with a cry. Coffee spilled across the bar, dripping down onto the floor. Her cats scattered with a pitched screech, disappearing under the armchair in the corner of the room. Grumbling, Beth went to fetch a towel.

As she trudged back, her phone began to ring. Ignoring it, she set about the arduous task of cleaning up spilled coffee; it had soaked into the wooden floor, staining it. Fantastic. The phone rang out. No voicemail. No sooner had she returned the towel to the sink when her phone started up again. Beth winced, but decided to answer anyway. It was probably work. A text never was enough-

An unknown number. The same one as before. The numbers glowed on her screen, mocking her. She should have ignored it, turned it off or blocked the number - but instead Beth raised it to her ear and called, "hello?"

"Beth."

Her chest skipped, her stomach flopped, and bile rose to the back of her throat. "Chandler."

"You've been ignoring my messages."

"Since when can you use a phone anyway," she snapped - and immediately slapped a hand over her lips. *Stupid!* "I'm sorry, I-" she cut herself off, eyes widening. Why was she *apologising* to him?

"I had to learn," he stated coldly, "how else could I contact you? You ran away from me Beth, without a word. How could you do that to me? To *Emily?*"

Suddenly the air felt frigid, too cold for a pleasant spring afternoon. Beth shivered, blinking back the first bubbles of tears. "How did you find me? I've seen you outside my house."

"I have my ways," he replied cryptically, "I came across states for you, Beth, and this is how you treat me?"

Pale hands curled around the phone. She wasn't going back. Not even if he tried to drag her kicking and screaming the entire way. She pursed her lips, silent. A single wrong move, one word he didn't like, and who knew what he might try.

"Our daughter misses you," Chandler laughed, "she's getting so big now, so *challenging*, but I know how to keep her in line-"

Fire rose in Beth's chest, hot and *painful* as she threw herself to her feet. "If you've hurt her, if you've even *thought* about it, I'll kill you!" That fire burned, threatening to spill over as she grasped the breakfast bar to tightly her knuckles turned white.

"If you're so worried about her, why did you leave? Come back to me Beth, you know it's where you belong."

Her entire body shook, free hand grasping at the corner of the bar like it was her lifeline. In truth, it was the only support keeping her from collapsing all together. She had *tried,* so desperately to take Emily with her but she was so young, so adamant she wanted to stay with Daddy and her grandparents.

This was all her fault.

"I've called the police," she warned, "you can't get away with this."

A low, rumbling laugh echoed through the distorted phone line. It made Beth shiver, made her flinch away. "And what will they do when they discover you abandoned your daughter? I doubt they will be sympathetic."

Beth's mind went numb. There was nothing to say, nothing except for half formed thoughts and the panic rising in her chest. The world seemed to freeze around her, narrowing until there was only her and Chandler's smug laughter ringing in her ears.

"I have her. Soon I'll have you too."

The phone slipped from her sweating hands, dropping to the floor with a thud and skittering away. The sound jolted her back to reality and she fumbled for it, shaking hands struggling to even pick it up. When she *finally* had it within her grasp again she sighed, heart pounding.

The call had ended. Chandler was gone. With him out of reach, so was her loving daughter.

It was impossible to know how long she sat huddled on the cold wooden floor, clutching her phone to her chest. Eventually her cats came to investigate, meowing softly. She pulled them both into a hug and buried her face into their soft fur. If she closed her eyes, it was almost possible to imagine it was the thick fluff of her daughter's golden hair.

———————————————

How **Matthew had convinced her to go out for lunch, Beth would never know. Three days of nothing from Chandler had only served to make her more paranoid - as was most likely his plan - and as they hours ticked by Beth found herself unable to concentrate on anything else. Yet when Matthew had convinced her, so sweet yet firm, that she needed to go outside, she had willingly accepted.**

The police are handling it, **he had said,** *worrying won't help.*

That was how Beth ended up in her favourite cafe holding a steaming latte between cold fingers as Matthew grinned at her from across the table. "I know you didn't want to come out today," he noted with a soft smile, "but I'm glad you did. Chandler wouldn't dare try anything in public."

It wasn't Matthew or herself she was concerned about; but Beth kept her lips sealed. What would he think of her if he knew she had abandoned her daughter? It wasn't as simple as that of course, but the thought of telling him made her stomach seize. "No one knows what he's capable of," she muttered, "not even me - but I don't want to think about him right now." Maybe it was selfish, wanting to enjoy a meal with her friend - date? she wasn't sure - but just for one day she wanted to *forget*.

Matthew nodded solemnly, but that gorgeous smile remained in place. Beth *liked* it when he smiled; it lit up the entire cafe, so bright and *honest*. It was breathtaking. With his sandy brown hair and dark eyes he wasn't her usual type; then again, with so little experience could Beth say she even had a type?

"Are you ready to order?"

Snapped out of her reverie, Beth jumped; and the chair screeched against the wooden floor. She flushed scarlet, head ducked low, but thankfully the waitress only smiled. They ordered, and when the pretty waitress left Beth finally allowed herself to breathe. She took a sip of her latte - scalding her tongue - just so she didn't have to look at Matthew.

"You're still thinking about Chandler." It wasn't a question.

Full lips pursed as Beth set down her coffee. "I don't *want* to think about him," she muttered, "but I can't stop. You don't know what he's like, Matthew. I didn't leave just because I felt like it."

"I know," Matthew murmured. His eyes dipped low, worried, and once again she was struck by just how *lovely* he was. "I'm sorry. I keep bringing it up, and I know I shouldn't-"

Beth's phone buzzed, deep within her handbag, and she jumped. She had been receiving texts all week from concerned friends so it wasn't anything unusual but... she shivered. When she reached inside her bag to pull out the phone her hands were clammy.

I've given you time to think. Will you return to me?

She blinked at the tiny screen, mind blank. Of course it was too much to want just *one day* without him on her mind. Her fingers tapped the screen, but what could she say? She wasn't going back to him, not *ever* - but what about Emily; her *daughter*?

He wouldn't hurt his own kid, she reasoned, but her stomach rolled.

"Something wrong?" Matthew questioned. Dark eyes darted from Beth's pale face to the phone, then back again. "Is he threatening you again?"

"No," she lied. "It's-"

Another text pinged through. Somehow, despite the sound being lost to the commotion of the busy cafe, it was too loud. *Deafening,* even, ringing in her ears like a bad omen. Beth didn't want to look. She *had* to look.

I'm here. She's with me.

Beth's heart shuddered, a gasp slipping from her lips before she had the chance to stop it. A pale hand flew to her face, the phone clattering onto the table. "He's at the house," was all she managed to say before the first tears slid down her face.

Matthew was on his feet in a flash, grabbing his coat and Beth's handbag without pause. "Call the police. You can stay at mine-"

"No!" Beth launched to her feet and coffee spilled across the table. An elderly couple turned to them with questioning eyes, lips curled in disgust. Beth only sent them a glare before turning to Matthew. "You can't get involved," she ordered, "I have to see him myself.

"You're not going to your house?" Matthew gasped, "stay with me until the police arrive."

"You don't understand," Beth hissed, voice low, "he has my *daughter*. She refused to come with me when I left. I should have made her, but I didn't. He has her and it's *my fault*."

Matthew regarded her silently, face unreadable - then he took her by the hand and murmured, "then let's go. Together."

They fled the cafe without paying, ignoring the confused calls of the waitress as they sprinted across the road. Still hand in hand they raced down the street without a care for passers by. The adrenaline coursed through Beth as her heart thundered. She was so tiny compared to Matthew but she practically dragged him the entire way back to the house.

The front door was locked - but as soon as Beth stood inside she saw how Chandler had got in; the hall window, too small for a man of his size to fit through, was just big enough for a ten year old. Emily. She had unlocked the Yale lock from inside.

"Where are they?" Matthew whispered. He crept in front of Beth as if to shield her, although no one was around. Beth clung to him anyway, fists curling around the soft fabric of his grey jacket.

Upstairs the floorboards creaked.

Beth's hands shook as she grabbed her phone. It nearly slipped from her hands twice but she managed to press emergency call.

"911. Do you need an ambulance, police or fire service?"

"Police," Beth whispered, "I've called before about... about my ex-husband. He's in my house and he has my daughter."

She zoned out, then, the calming voice of the 911 operator sinking into the background as wide eyes snapped to the stairs. Without the lights on they were washed in darkness, no upstairs windows to illuminate them. The shadows shifted and she saw only a broad face surrounded by a shock of blonde hair.

Chandler.

"Where's Emily?" Beth demanded. Her voice wobbled and tears threatened to spill; not that she had wiped away the previous ones. "Did you hurt her?"

His smirk revealed perfect white teeth; and once his smile had made her heart melt. That hadn't been in a long, *long* time. "I wouldn't hurt my own child," he stated, "what kind of monster do

you think I am?"

"One that beats his wife," Matthew snapped, "and uses his daughter as leverage." He spread his long arms, blocking Chandler from Beth's view just long enough to make her heart stutter. Chandler was slow, a real brute, but taking her eyes off of him for a *second* made her nauseous.

When Beth peeked around Matthew's shoulders he tried to nudge her back, but Beth held firm. "Where's Emily? I need to see her-"

"I'll allow you to see her," Chandler snarled, "if you agree to come back home with me."

Beth froze. Her pulse raced and her throat constricted - but all she had to do was play along until the police arrived. Swallowing down her fear, Beth nodded. "All right. I will."

"Beth, wait-"

She shot Matthew a narrow eyed glare and blinked back the onslaught of tears. "I need to see my daughter," she told him. Silently, she hoped he was smart enough to understand.

Beth only made it two steps before Chandler wrapped her up in his broad arms. It was suffocating, overwhelming, and Beth had to fight the urge to shove him away. Instead she wrapped her arms around him too, even as her skin *crawled*.

"I love you Beth. You know that, right?"

Beth couldn't force herself to reply. Instead she whispered, "take me to

Emily."

"Upstairs."

Beth scrambled away from him the second he freed her from his vice-like grasp - but even then he wasn't done. His enormous body hovered so close he breathed down her neck as she ascended the stairs, into the darkness. Matthew tried to follow - but a warning from Chandler stopped him in his tracks.

And there she was. Tiny Emily curled up on Beth's bed, bundled in her coat. Her head snapped up as Beth entered and the relief that washed over her was *palpable*. Or perhaps it was Beth's own relief at seeing her daughter after two long years. Emily's hair was longer and her little body beneath the layers was taller, but otherwise she looked exactly as she remembered.

Beth rushed to her. Emily clambered from the bed and ran into Beth's outstretched arms with a cry of, "I missed you!" and buried her face in Beth's blonde curls.

"What a happy reunion," Chandler murmured. He crouched by the two and wrapped a thick arm around Beth's shoulders. She had to force down the urge to flinch. "Now we can all be together, back home where we belong."

Emily's lips quivered, but she didn't say a word. She had always been quiet, but this kind of silence opened up a pit in Beth's stomach. "You promise you haven't hurt Emily?"

A low growl and Chandler's grip around her thin shoulders tightened. Painfully. "She's such a good girl. Quiet, nothing I can't

handle. I only hurt those that *deserve it.*"

Tears prickled her eyes and she turned. Emily didn't need to see this. Her lips parted, although she was barely aware of what she intended to say.

There was no chance to speak, not when the wail of police sirens sliced through her thoughts, left her mind whirling. *About time.*

"You called the police?" Chandler roared, storming to his feet. Beth scrambled to her feet, holding Emily close, just as Chandler's fists tightened.

Then she was darting down the stairs, Emily's legs bouncing against her hip - and without thinking she ran right into Matthew's arms. "They're here," she breathed - and for the first time in so long, *hope* blossomed in her chest.

The three stepped aside as police stormed the little house. Emily stood silently by her mother's side and they both stared with wide, thankful eyes as the police carted Chandler from the house. He kicked, throwing threats across the hall, promising to come for them both.

By the time the police had finally taken their statements, by the time silence flooded the house and everyone was gone, Beth was ready to collapse. Somehow Emily had managed to fall asleep in the living room, a blanket tucked neatly around her, and Beth wished she was ready to do the same.

Matthew perched on the sofa as Beth all but collapsed beside him. "You can sleep at mine tonight," he said softly, "I have a spare room for you and Emily."

"You've already done so much for us," she murmured. Even so, she didn't know if it was possible to sleep here tonight. Did she even want to try?

"I care about you," Matthew murmured. When had he leaned in so close? Had their knees always been touching? "I want you to feel safe. Please, stay with me tonight."

With me. For some reason those words stuck in her mind, replaying over and over. Beth didn't even know she had closed the distance between them until she crushed her lips to his. She smiled against his full lips, eyes fluttering closed - but then she realised she had crossed a line. Fumbling she broke free of the kiss, an apology rising in her throat-

Matthew pulled her back, hands tangling in her thick blonde hair. He kissed her gently, tenderly, but there was no doubt in her mind that he *meant it*. When they pulled away her cheeks were flushed, laughter on her lips. Matthew grinned back, his own cheeks barely pink.

"I admit I didn't expect that," he murmured, biting back laughter.

"Me neither," Beth admitted. She would have been embarrassed if Matthew's gaze wasn't so soft, so affectionate. She shifted, eager to kiss him again but conscious of Emily sleeping close by.

"You know I'm here for you, don't you? Emily too."

"Matthew," she protested, "I can't expect you to-"

"I want to. I want to make sure he never touches you again, make sure you're safe."

With a smile on her lips Beth ducked in for another gentle kiss. After a moment she sank into it, into Matthew, allowing him to wrap his arms around her waist and pull her close. The exhaustion took over and suddenly it was impossible just to keep her eyes open.

As Beth drifted off to the first peaceful sleep in weeks, she finally knew that everything was okay.

AMISH HIDEAWAY

STEPHANIE SWIFT

Anna Brenneman hummed softly and smiled as she scribbled homework instructions on the blackboard. It was finally Friday. Only three more weeks remained of the school year term, and that fact was more than evident by her student's behavior. Everyone was excited and anxious for the term to come to an end, and that resulted in less concentration on schoolwork and more attention on talking about summer plans. Not that she could blame them because she was ready for a much-needed break too.

"Okay, class...Monday we'll be working on the last group project before your final exams, so I need everyone to divide up into groups of four," she said.

It didn't take much prompting for the children to jump from their seats and gravitate to their best friends. As usual, the boys stuck together in their little cliques, and so did the girls, but Anna noticed one student, eight-year-old Hope Roth, still sitting at her desk, busily drawing something on a piece of paper. She seemed oblivious to everything happening around her.

"Hope?" she called.

Still no reaction.

"Okay, everyone, I want you to move your desks into a circle pattern with your group, so you can work together on ideas for your project. Try to do it quietly!"

As the others did as they were told, Anna walked over to Hope's desk and knelt beside it.

"Hope, sweetie, what are you doing?" she asked.

She glanced at Hope's paper and discovered she'd drawn a photo of a table with a tall pitcher of lemonade and glasses sitting on top of it, and "Lemonade: 25 cents" was scrawled in huge letters at the top of the page.

"My *daed* is going to build a stand for me like this one so I can sell lemonade this summer and make some money for us."

Anna cringed. Why would any adult ask a eight-year-old to take on a job, even something as small as selling lemonade at a roadside stand? She knew that Hope and her father had fallen on some hard times in the wake of her mother's passing from cancer many months prior, but she had no idea it had gotten so bad.

"That's nice, Hope, but I need you to put your colors away so you can focus on the project we're working on for next week. Will you do that for me?"

Hope hung her head and pursed her lips.

"Do I have to, Miss Brenneman? I'd rather work on my lemonade business."

It sounded so strange and very sad hearing grown-up words coming from such a small child. Part of her wanted to let her forego the project because her "business" seemed so important to her, but she knew it wouldn't be fair to the other children if she showed favoritism. After much persuading, she managed to talk Hope into joining three other girls in the classroom who needed one more participant to form their group, but she didn't seem happy about it at all.

Her heart ached as she watched Hope lay her head down on her desk and half-heartedly listen to the other girls plan the outline for their project. It bothered her greatly when any of her students were hurting, but knowing the sadness Hope had endured since her mother's death made her situation even more disconcerting.

Anna made a mental note to speak to her father about it when he picked her up after school, but at the end of the day, while she was busy putting away her classroom supplies, Anna glanced out one of the school building windows and noticed Hope walking the dirt road home with Ivy and Leah, two other classmates.

Anna walked outside where a couple of the other children were waiting to be picked up. She saw a horse-drawn wagon approaching from the opposite direction, but it wasn't being driven by Hope's father.

"Thomas, have you seen Mr. Caleb Roth?"

The young boy, who was close in age to Hope, shrugged his shoulders. "Hope said he must have forgotten, so she decided to walk home with Ivy and Leah."

He said it so nonchalantly, as if Hope's father forgetting to pick up his daughter from school was no big deal, but it made Anna angry. Who forgets to pick up their child from school? She tried to rationalize it. Perhaps something happened to delay him. The thought made her pulse race, and she prayed he wasn't hurt. Hope was already struggling with losing her mother. Losing both her parents would be devastating.

Anna tried to push the troubling thought from her mind. It was probably something unavoidable that couldn't be helped, and there was no reason to jump to conclusions or think the worst. Still, as she returned to her classroom and continued putting things away, she couldn't shake the gnawing feeling that something wasn't right.

* * * *

Caleb Roth pulled on the reins and brought his plow horse to a stop when a bright glimmer in the distance caught his attention. Shielding his eyes from the sun with his hand, he tried to locate where the glare was coming from, and his heart dropped to his feet when he spotted his daughter, Hope, walking the dirt road toward their house. The sun danced off her metal lunch pail, and he groaned and hung his head in shame.

He'd forgotten again.

It was the second time in the past two months he'd forgotten to pick Hope up from school, and he felt like kicking himself. Caleb dropped the reins and walked over to the wooden fence lining the pasture to greet her. When she caught sight of him, she took off running in his direction, her long blonde braid bouncing behind her and a smile lighting up her angelic little face.

Caleb sighed. She looked so much like her mother when she smiled, with their matching dimples and big, soulful brown eyes. As much as he loved her taking after Abigail, he couldn't deny that there were moments when the similarities gripped his heart and squeezed like a vise. When she got to the fence, she put her schoolbooks and lunch pail on the ground and climbed the fence so she could hug him.

"I'm so sorry I forgot to pick you up from school. I started plowing, and I just lost track of time. Can you forgive me?"

She gave him a curious look and giggled, as if he'd just said the funniest thing.

"Of course, I can," she said. "It's okay. I had fun walking with Ivy and Leah. Did you know that Ivy's sister, Clara, is getting married next month? Their mom is making her dress, and I bet it's going to be beautiful!"

He smiled at her comment, although a part of him ached when he considered the many things she would miss out on as she got older, including Abigail designing her own wedding dress. He knew God had a reason for taking her so soon, but he still didn't understand it and probably never would.

"Oh! I drew something for you today," she exclaimed.

She jumped off the fence long enough to retrieve a piece of paper from one of her school books.

"Can you build this for me, *daed*? I want to sell lemonade this summer, and Leah said I could probably put it on the sidewalk outside her mom's quilt shop in town, if that's okay with you."

He unfolded the piece of paper, and his heart melted when he saw the colored wooden stand and several stick figure people holding glasses of lemonade. She also drew a likeness of her behind the stand, complete with brown eyes and a long braid in her blonde hair.

"I'm sure I can probably come up with something that will work," he replied.

Hope clapped her hands together excitedly and leaned over the fence so she could kiss his cheek.

"Why don't you go clean up and do your homework while I finish up here? I'll check it when I come inside, and we'll get started on dinner, so we can discuss this lemonade stand of yours."

She nodded and smiled before picking up her supplies and running toward the house. Caleb looked at the drawing one more time before folding it up neatly and putting it inside his shirt pocket.

"She's got your eye for business, Abigail," he said softly, as he looked up at the blue sky and rolling clouds. "I know you'd be proud."

* * * *

Anna tapped her fingers against her knee as she and Hope sat on the front steps outside the schoolhouse the following afternoon. Thirty minutes had passed and all the other children had gone home, but Hope's father still hadn't shown. Anna felt her temper steadily rise as she watched Hope aimlessly sift through one of her textbooks.

"Okay, this is ridiculous," she stated. "Come on, Hope. I'm taking you home."

Thankfully, Hope didn't put up a fuss, and in no time at all, they were tucked away inside Anna's horse-drawn buggy and heading for the Roth homestead. Anna tried to keep her anger at bay, but there was no justifiable reason for any parent to forget their child, and someone needed to speak up on Hope's behalf.

She went over the conversation in her mind repeatedly, trying to figure out a way to approach the subject gracefully, but there was no use. She was upset and Caleb Roth was going to find out soon enough just what she thought about his parenting skills, or lack thereof.

When she steered the horse and buggy into Hope's driveway ten minutes later, she caught sight of him plowing the pasture behind their home. As soon as he saw them, he stopped what he was doing and walked over to greet them. Besides the casual "hello" at church, and the wave he sometimes gave her when he did decide to pick Hope up from school, they'd never formally spoken to each other.

As he drew closer, she couldn't help but notice his unkempt wavy brown hair and the dust that littered his clothes. His long-sleeved shirt was unbuttoned at the wrists and rolled to the elbows, and the top two buttons of his shirt were undone, revealing a thin sheen of perspiration on his chest. For some reason, the messiness in his physical appearance worked together to create something very rugged and masculine, and Anna caught herself staring. Shaking her head to clear her thoughts, she tried to avert her attention elsewhere.

"Miss Brenneman, I'm truly sorry. I had a problem with my plow earlier, and once I got it repaired and started plowing, I forgot the time. Thank you so much for bringing Hope home. It won't happen again. I give you my word."

Hope dropped the reins and laced her hands on top of her lap. She had no choice but to look at him, and when she gazed into his mesmerizing green eyes, she almost tripped over her own tongue.

"Mr. Roth, I need to speak to you...alone."

Something in the tone of her voice must have caught him off guard, because he gave her a skeptical look before motioning to Hope to wait for him inside the house. When she did as he asked, he stuffed the handkerchief he was holding inside his pants pocket and crossed his arms over his chest.

"Is there something you would like to say to me, Miss Brenneman?"

She did her best to remain calm by reminding herself that he was the parent of one of her students, and she shouldn't cause trouble, but the condescending expression on his face changed that in a heartbeat. He looked like he might even start laughing, which infuriated her even more.

"Mr. Roth..."

He shook his head. "Please call me Caleb."

Anna cleared her throat. "Fine," she began again. "*Caleb*, I understand that you and Hope have had a difficult year since your wife's passing, and I am sincerely sorry for your loss, but Hope already deals with enough worries without having to wonder every day if her father is going to pick her up from school or not."

He uncrossed his arms and pressed a hand against the side of her buggy to prop himself up.

"Excuse me? What other worries do you *think* Hope has...not that losing her mother isn't enough?"

He squinted his eyes, and she could tell by the tempered sound of his voice that he was probably trying to maintain his composure, but she was past the point of caring. Hope stood and descended the steps of her buggy. When Caleb attempted to help her, she pushed his hand away. When they were standing face to face, she was suddenly struck with how tall and broad-shouldered he was, but she wasn't about to cower in front of him. If David could stand against Goliath, then she could do the same with Caleb Roth.

"As if you don't know?" she asked. "What parent asks their eight-year-old child to work all summer selling lemonade to help pay the family bills? Do you really think that's appropriate?"

Caleb took a step back, and he genuinely looked surprised by her comment because he didn't say anything for the longest while. When he did speak, his voice was much softer and calmer. His shoulders slumped and he seemed almost sad...defeated even.

"Miss Brenneman, I can assure you that I've never asked Hope to work to support us. I manage that fine on my own. She did ask me yesterday if I would build her a stand so she could sell lemonade in town this summer, but I thought she wanted to earn a little extra money to buy something new for herself."

Anna wasn't sure how to reply. She didn't know the man personally, but she could usually tell when someone was lying to her, and he wasn't lying.

"Perhaps you should get the whole story before you start passing judgement on me or anyone else for that matter," he remarked.

She probably should have apologized, but he stood up straight again and towered over her, which bristled her nerves. They were standing so close she could barely breathe.

"Have you ever lost someone close to you, Miss Brenneman?"

She put her hands on her hips and held her chin high. "No, I haven't, but I don't see what that has to do with any of this."

He continued glaring a hole straight through her, but she refused to back down.

"Since my wife died, I've been trying very hard to run our home as smoothly as she once did, but that isn't easy. I get up an hour early each morning so I can cook Hope breakfast before I take her to school. I spend the rest of the day dividing my time between washing our clothes and tending to other household chores and getting my work done on our farm so I can afford to put food on our table and pay the bills. My wife always did such a wonderful job making our house a home, and somehow she even managed to have her own vegetable garden in our backyard too, and she would tend to it daily and sell her crops to clients in town."

His speech was so impassioned, she didn't dare interrupt, not that he would have given her the opportunity.

"Every night I cook our dinner before helping Hope with her homework. When she goes to sleep, I clean the kitchen and mend any clothes that need mending. I usually go to sleep around midnight. I don't mind doing any of this though because I'm her father, and I love her more than life itself, and it's my responsibility to take care of her. Still, it's not easy, and unless you've been in my shoes, then I politely ask you to stop judging me. God Almighty is my only judge – not you."

By the time he finished speaking, he was standing so close their bodies were almost touching, and he was looking down on her with fire in his eyes and his breathing was labored. She thought about what he said, and she hated to admit that he was right. She'd never been married – or in love, for that matter. It was easy to see the depth of his love for his late wife by the way he talked about her, and she couldn't help but wonder what that must feel like – to love someone with such passion and heartfelt emotion.

Her plan to teach Caleb a lesson had backfired on her, and she felt ashamed and full of remorse. Hot tears sprang to her eyes, and she knew it would be best to retreat before she started crying – something she *did not* want him to witness.

Anna adjusted the bonnet on her head and flattened the apron on her long dress before attempting to speak.

"You're right, Caleb, and I apologize for misjudging you. It won't happen again."

She tried to ascend the steps on her buggy, but he reached out and stopped her by lightly grasping her arm.

"Anna..."

His voice was soft and soothing and the heat from his touch seared through the fabric of her dress and warmed her blood. Still, she refused to look at him, and when she jerked her arm from his grasp, he didn't try to dissuade her from leaving. Anna took her place behind the reins and steered the horse and buggy onto the main dirt road. Once she was finally out of view of Caleb, she let her tears fall where they may.

* * * *

Caleb sat at the kitchen table the next morning, mindlessly turning his coffee mug around and around on top of the wooden table...and trying not to think about Anna Brenneman.

He groaned.

It was pointless. He hadn't been able to sleep all night because every time he closed his eyes he would picture her standing in front of him with tears in her beautiful blue eyes after he berated her for insinuating he was a bad father.

He felt horrible for hurting her feelings. He knew she was just worried over her student, like any good teacher would be. After discovering the real reason Hope wanted him to build a lemonade stand, he felt as if someone had kicked him in the gut, and even though he knew he was just defending himself, he still could have been a gentleman and handled his answers with more tact.

Had he really made Hope feel like she needed a job to help support the two of them? Was he failing her somehow? The thought that he might be disappointing her in some way made his heart ache. She'd already been through so much since losing Abigail. He would never dream of putting her through anymore sorrow.

"*Daed*?"

Caleb turned to find Hope entering the kitchen, rubbing her eyes and shuffling her feet on the floor as she walked.

"Is it time for breakfast?" she asked before stifling a yawn.

Caleb stretched out his arms and she walked over to join him and climbed on top of his lap. When she rested her head on his shoulder, he kissed her forehead and rocked her back and forth, the way he used to when she was a baby.

"Not yet, sweetheart. What are you doing up so early? You still have another couple of hours before you have to get ready for school."

She yawned again. "I saw the light from the lantern, and I wanted to make sure you were okay."

He squeezed her tight.

"You worry too much about me. I'm fine."

She smiled. "That's what I'm supposed to do."

Caleb chuckled at her remark. "No, you should be focusing on what all eight-year-old girls love doing, like playing with your friends and your dolls. I don't want you to ever think that it's your job to take care of me. Miss Brenneman told me you want to sell lemonade this summer to make money for us, and you don't have to do that because I've got that under control. Any money you make will go towards buying something *you* want. Okay?"

She nodded and wrapped her little arms around his neck and held on tight. He expelled a peaceful sigh. These were the moments he cherished the most.

"I'm just doing what mom asked me to do," she said.

Caleb furrowed a brow at her comment and pulled her back so he could look at her more closely.

"What do you mean? What did mom ask you to do?"

Hope smiled up at him. "Before she went to be with Jesus, she asked me to make sure you weren't sad all the time after she left. She wants you to be happy, and I want you to be happy too."

Caleb didn't know what to say. There were so many different emotions swirling through his heart and mind, he felt overwhelmed and unsure if he could even speak at all. He had no doubt Abigail did just as Hope described. She was always thinking about other people instead of herself, even in her darkest hours.

Hope kissed his cheek before going back to her bedroom, but Caleb kept his place. He couldn't sleep even if he really wanted to. He thought a lot about Abigail's wishes and perhaps she was right. Maybe it *was* time for him to be happy again. Although he had everything a man could possibly dream of – his faith in God, a nice home, a good paying job, and a healthy child – there was still something missing and he knew what that was. It wasn't just the physical closeness with a woman he missed. More than anything else, it was the companionship shared between two people who love each other that he missed the most.

Caleb looked out the kitchen window over the sink as the sun prepared to make its debut. He knew the steps he needed to take to have that again, but he worried he might be too rusty to give it another try. After all, it had been many years since he courted a woman.

Caleb propped his elbows on the kitchen table, laced his fingers together, and bowed his head in prayer. *Lord, you know what's on my heart and my mind. I pray for your strength and guidance and for your will to be done in mine and Hope's lives. Amen.*

* * * *

Anna closed her songbook and laid it in her lap as the Bishop took his place behind the podium to preach. She glanced quickly around the crowded room to see who was in attendance, and it looked as if everyone from their small community was there. Church days were always day-long events amongst the Amish people, and Anna looked forward to seeing the friends she didn't normally see during the week.

"Someone is staring at you."

She looked to her left at her close friend, Karen, who whispered in her ear. She followed Karen's gaze to a far corner of the room where Caleb Roth was sitting. Hope sat beside him, but instead of watching the Bishop, his eyes were on her, and they didn't waver when she caught him staring at her. It felt like a battle of wills, waiting to see who would look away first, and she didn't know whether to feel excited or afraid.

He didn't look angry. It was hard to tell exactly what emotion was dancing across his handsome face. He was a difficult man to figure out. When the Bishop cleared his throat, obviously for her attention, Anna tore her gaze from Caleb and put her focus where it should be, on the Bishop's sermon.

When Karen giggled, Anna elbowed her in the side to make her stop. The heat rose to her cheeks, and when the Bishop turned back to his sermon, she vowed then and there to stop fretting over Caleb Roth. What good could come of it anyway? *Yah*, he was a handsome, hardworking man, but his heart was still bound to a cemetery plot on the outskirts of town and that would probably never change.

After the service, the women began preparing for the noon meal while the men set up tables and chairs beneath a large grove of oaks trees beside the church. Anna was thankful for the reprieve, and she kept her eyes on the task at hand and didn't let anything deter her.

When the meal was ready, and the Bishop gave thanks, she sat at a table with Karen and two other single women from their community. Several of the children she taught in school stopped by her table to say hello, including Hope, but Anna noticed right away Caleb wasn't with her, and that bothered her more than she would ever admit to.

After the meal, when the food was put away and the tables were cleared, everyone started making their way inside the church once again for the Bishop's afternoon sermon. As Anna walked beside Karen, she felt someone tap her on the shoulder, and her heart skipped a beat, hoping it might be Caleb, but it was Gabriel Conrad, a single father to two of her students.

"*Guder nammidaag*, Miss Brenneman."

Karen gave her a sly wink before leaving her side to join the others in the church.

"*Guder nammidaag*, Mr. Conrad. How are you?"

He took off his hat and held it with both hands.

"I'm doing well. Thank you."

He looked positively frightened, but she had no idea why. She noticed his three children standing several feet away, and they all smiled and waved to her, but they kept their place.

"Mr. Conrad, is something wrong?" she inquired. "Are the children having problems with their schoolwork?"

He shook his head and she noticed his forehead was covered in tiny beads of perspiration. He swallowed and cleared his throat.

"Oh no, no. They're doing great," he replied. "I was just wondering...I wanted to ask if you would like to have dinner with me sometime."

To say Anna was stunned would be an understatement. It wasn't that she didn't appreciate his offer, but he was several years older than her, so his invitation surprised her. His oldest child had already completed school and his youngest two weren't far behind. Still, she hated to be rude and decline, especially since it was obvious it took a lot of courage for him to ask in the first place.

"That would be nice. Thank you," she replied.

He seemed extremely relieved by her answer, and as they fell in step with each other and briefly discussed a day and time on their trek to the church, she noticed Caleb standing at the top of the wooden steps leading to the front door. He was watching her intently, but she didn't acknowledge him when she walked by and he didn't attempt to do the same.

Maybe it was better this way, since she'd already made a bad impression and caused enough trouble with him. As she and Gabriel parted ways, and she took her seat beside Karen, she couldn't shake the empty feeling deep inside her heart. Something was missing and she didn't know what. Perhaps she never would.

* * * *

Caleb sat atop his wagon and stared at the schoolhouse. It was the last day of school, and it also felt like his last chance. After today, he wouldn't see Anna every weekday, and that thought had a grip on his heart he couldn't shake. He would only see her a couple of times a month at church unless he found the courage to speak up now before it was too late...which it very well could be.

When the front doors opened a few minutes later, and the kids ran outside jumping and rejoicing over the beginning of their summer break, he smiled when he saw Hope ambling her way over to him. Caleb jumped down from the wagon and met her halfway.

"I'm surprised you aren't celebrating with the other kids," he said.

Hope glimpsed their way and shrugged her shoulders. "They may be happy, but I'm going to miss school."

She looked so pitiful when she said it, and Caleb picked her up and gave her a big hug before setting her feet back on the ground.

"Sweetie, would you mind staying out here a few minutes while I go talk to Miss Brenneman?"

Hope's sad frown turned upside down and her face lit up.

"I'll be on the swing!" she yelled, before darting off in the direction of the tire swing hanging from a pine tree beside the school.

Caleb climbed the steps and took a long, deep breath before opening the front door. He expected Hope to be alone, but two of her students lingered behind the others, and she was sitting at her desk, showing them something in a textbook. She looked up when the door opened, and she gave him a halfhearted smile before turning her attention back to the students.

He sighed. This was going to be harder than he imagined. She was obviously still angry over their confrontation at his house, and he wondered if they would ever be able to get past it. He walked slowly around the room, admiring the children's artwork tacked to the walls and trying to look busy. When her students finally left, the small space became so quiet you could hear a pin drop. Anna stood and walked over to the blackboard.

"Can I help you with something, Mr. Roth?"

He rolled his eyes heavenward. They were back to formalities again. He made his way over to her and stood patiently by as she erased the board. She looked so beautiful in her long blue dress. Her hair was gathered into a bun on top of her head, but several tendrils had escaped and now caressed her cheeks and neck. He took off his hat and gripped it hard with both hands so he wouldn't be tempted to touch her. The longing he'd felt for her since their first meeting stirred deep inside him, and he swallowed hard to try and remain calm and collected.

"Anna, please look at me."

She stopped and put the eraser down, but she didn't turn to face him right away. When she did, he noticed her expression had grown softer and she even smiled at him.

"I need to apologize," he began. "I shouldn't have spoken to you the way I did when you came to my house to ask about Hope. I'm thankful for your concern for her, and I'm sorry for my behavior."

Anna hung her head and shuffled her feet against the wooden floor.

"You shouldn't apologize to me, Caleb. I should be the one apologizing. I was angry during the drive to your house, and I should have waited and found out the facts before I started jumping to conclusions. You were right...about everything."

He looked out the window at Hope playing on the tire swing and he smiled.

"I asked Hope a little while ago why she wasn't celebrating being out for summer break like the other kids were doing, and she said it was because she's going to miss school, but what I really think she meant is she's going to miss you. I have to admit that the thought of not seeing you as often bothers me too."

She looked up at him, and it was obvious by her expression that his comment surprised her. He placed his hat on top of her desk and closed the gap between them.

"Am I too late, Anna?"

She tilted her head and gave him a curious look. "Too late for what?"

He reached out and held one of her hands, and he marveled at the softness of her skin. He also smiled when he noticed the effect he was having on her when he felt her body tremble.

"Is it too late for us to create a new beginning? To pretend that our misunderstanding never happened and start over?" he asked. "I saw you talking to Gabriel Conrad a few days ago, and I don't want to interfere if there is something between the two of you."

Anna laughed softly and shook her head. "There's nothing to interfere. We had one date, and I quickly realized we weren't mean to be together, but we parted as friends."

He tried not to let on how relieved he was by the news, but it felt like a huge burden had been lifted from his heart. Since seeing the two of them talking at church, he hadn't been able to concentrate on anything else. He knew Gabriel Conrad very well. He was searching for a wife to help raise his three children, and Caleb had the feeling it didn't matter to Gabriel whether they were compatible or not. He wanted a maid and cook – not a helpmate and companion. He felt the need to warn her, but he also knew it wasn't his place to stick his nose where it didn't belong, so instead he prayed fervently for her to come to the same conclusion herself, which apparently, she must have.

"Does that mean we can officially start over then?" he asked.

When she nodded in return, he let go of her hand and took a few steps back. He grabbed his hat from the desk and put it back on before clearing his throat. He tipped his hat to her and smiled.

"Hello, Miss Brenneman. My name is Caleb Roth. It's so nice meeting you."

He reached out and took her hand, and when he brought it to his lips, he tried not to grin when he noticed how her bottom lip quivered.

"It's nice meeting you too, Mr. Roth, but please call me Anna."

He stepped closer until there was barely enough space left between them to breathe. He could detect a faint whisper of lavender in her hair and on her skin, and he breathed in deeply, savoring the scent.

"Anna," he whispered. "Would you please do me the honor of letting me take you out on a date?"

He didn't know if it was the closeness of their bodies that made her unable to speak or something else, but she blushed before nodding. Happiness flooded his heart, and perhaps he was taking a risk, but he wanted to kiss her so badly, and he knew if he didn't he would lose his nerve.

Caleb brushed his fingertips against her cheek before leaning over and briefly pressing his lips to her own. It may have lasted only a few seconds, but the impact of it lingered as he felt a surge of heat rush through his veins and warm his blood. Every part of his body ached to kiss her again, only this time more earnestly, but he also didn't want to risk scaring her away, so he moved away from her slightly to try and ease the temptation.

Suddenly the front door burst open and Hope was running toward them. At first, it frightened him, thinking something must have happened to her while she was outside, but when she drew closer, he noticed the enormous smile on her face.

"I saw it!" she exclaimed. "I saw you kissing!"

Caleb sucked in a breath, having totally forgotten she was right outside the window on the tire swing. He glanced at Anna, who also looked very nervous.

"Does this mean I'll be seeing you a lot this summer?" Hope asked.

Caleb and Anna exchanged a knowing glance.

"Would you be okay with that?" Anna replied.

Hope clapped her hands together excitedly and ran behind the desk so she could wrap her arms around them both. "Yes!"

Anna stood on her tiptoes so she could whisper in Caleb's ear.

"It looks like you have yourself a date, Mr. Roth."

He kissed her forehead and grinned. "And I hope it's the first of many."

AMISH COMPLICATIONS
MONICA MARKS

The Choice

Her father cautiously steered the horse into the parking lot and Rachel gathered her things.

Her mother refused to look at her as she stepped from the cart, but she could see how white were her lips as they pursed together in anger.

"*Mammi*," Rachel said imploringly. "It is just a – "

"You do what you must, Rachel," Ruth interjected sternly, her green eyes still averted. "You are my daughter and I will love you regardless of what you choose."

Rachel swallowed the lump forming in her throat and glanced at her father desperately.

Daniel tried to smile weakly, but the expression seemed more of a grimace.

"Hurry along now, *liebchen*. You will be late," he told her, but Rachel knew it had less to do with her tardiness and more that he worried Ruth would fully speak her mind.

Rachel stifled a sigh and smoothed out her skirt, peering toward the building.

Perhaps they will go with someone else, she thought, the idea filling her with hope and disappointment simultaneously.

The problem was, Rachel didn't know what she wanted, not exactly.

Ever since Jacob and Lovina had announced their engagement two weeks earlier, Rachel had suddenly been lost in a void.

She felt like she was walking along in a never-ending dream, one which she would eventually wake and find that her best friend and secret love were not marrying in the coming year.

But it was no dream and Rachel knew she would never wake up.

As long as she remained in the district, Rachel was bound to live in the shadow of Jacob and Lovina's affections.

Rachel was also aware that the decision to interview for the teaching job at the elementary school in Holmesville was one which was breaking her parents' hearts, but Rachel was sure she could not spend one more minute in the district, knowing she would eventually see the newly betrothed couple anywhere and without warning.

This is your own doing, she reminded herself as she hurried toward the front of the school. *If you had made your feelings known, maybe Jacob would have chosen you. If you had said something, perhaps Lovina would not have fallen in love with him.*

It was a silly game of "what if" which she could not seem to stop playing with herself and Rachel had to separate herself from the heartbreak she was feeling.

But it was done and there was little she could do, not now. Even if things did not work out between Lovina and Jacob, he would be untouchable to her, Lovina's friend.

Rachel had missed her opportunity and it was gone forever.

Of course she had not explained her decision to her parents. They did not understand why she was preparing to leave the community when she had always expressed a desire to be baptized and embrace the *Ordnung.*

I am sure this will only be temporary, Rachel told herself as she entered the structure and walked into the office, presenting the most pleasing smile she could muster. *I will miss my home out here among the Englisch and go running home.*

Rachel also had to face the fact that she was assuming she got the job as a teaching assistant in the small school.

"May I help you?"

The receptionist peered at her through spectacles perched at the edge of a bird-like nose. Her lips seemed to form a slash as she studied the dark-haired woman in homespun clothes.

"I have an interview with Principal Cotton," Rachel explained. "My name is Rachel Littwiller."

"An interview for what?" the woman demanded, and Rachel noted the name on her plaque read "Amy Wheeler."

"A teaching assistant," Rachel replied quietly, her back tensing slightly at the open expression of disdain on Amy's face.

Do they not keep calendars with appointments? Can she not just look at the time slot?

Of course Rachel did not speak her questions aloud.

"*Teaching assistant?*" Amy echoed, arching a thin, painted eyebrow. "Really? Are you sure?"

Rachel did not know how to respond to the woman's open skepticism but before she could say a word, the door to the inner office opened and a robust man in his fifties exited.

"Ah! You must be Ms. Littwiller! Please, come in. You're right on time."

Rachel exhaled slowly, grateful that Principal Cotton seemed more amiable than his sour-faced receptionist.

"Good luck," Amy said snidely, a snicker in her voice and Rachel's brow creased.

Why is she being so hostile toward me? She does not know the first thing about me.

She did not have time to pursue the concern as Principal Cotton ushered her into the room and gestured for her to sit down.

"I am so happy to meet you, Rachel. Bishop Miller and I have been friends for many years and he speaks so highly of you. Although I must say this is the first time he has ever recommended anyone in the district for a teaching position."

Rachel peered at him with vivid green eyes, searching for the right words.

"He is a good man, Bishop Miller," she finally offered. "And I appreciate you taking the time to meet with me."

Principal Cotton nodded in agreement.

"That is why I trust him wholeheartedly when he suggested you. We are thrilled to have you onboard at Thomas Jefferson Elementary."

She gazed at him, shocked.

Is he hiring me without so much as an interview? Based on Bishop Miller's word?

"You have already made your decision then?" she breathed, a combination of happiness and dread sweeping over her.

"Unless you have anything you would like to discuss before we sign the paperwork," he replied, smiling broadly. He opened a manila folder and began shuffling through a pile of papers.

Rachel shook her head, stunned at what she was seeing.

The papers are simply ready to be signed! I got the job!

"No!" she cried. "Thank you very much! I will not disappoint you!"

Principal Cotton chuckled.

"That is the last thing I worried about," he assured her, extending his hand. "You will start on Monday. Classes commence at eight a.m., but you may wish to be here early, so you are able to discuss your duties with Mrs. Verhoot. That is whose class you will be assisting. Have you any questions at all for me, Rachel?"

She gulped, thousands of words flooding her mind, but she could not formulate a proper question.

Instead, she shook her long black braid and accepted his outstretched palm.

"Thank you!" she said again, realizing she had already thanked him profusely but she could not think of anything else to say.

Principal Cotton beamed.

"You have earned it," he said jovially, pushing the pages toward her to sign. The next few minutes consisted of Rachel writing her signature, but she was too overwhelmed to notice what she was signing.

It was not until Rachel was back at the wagon where her parents waited did she wonder what it was she had done to deserve the job.

Surely there are others more qualified than me, she thought. *Ones with more education or experience...*

"What did he say?" Daniel asked as they started back toward the district.

He was the first one to break the silence in the wagon, Rachel lost in thought over what had happened and how fast it had occurred.

Rachel's excitement was fleeting as she realized she had to break the news to her parents.

"I have the job," she murmured, trying to keep the glee from her voice.

Ruth stifled a sob, but Daniel gave her a rueful smile.

"I had no doubt you would get it," he told her. "They are fortunate to have you. The children in the district adore you."

Rachel eyed him gratefully, but the rest of the trip home was made in silence as each family member was consumed with their own thoughts.

Rachel was already wondering if she had made a mistake but as Daniel guided the cart back toward their house, she noticed a couple walking up the road.

As they drew closer, Rachel's heart froze in her chest.

It was Lovina and Jacob, their heads close as they seemed lost in conversation.

At the last minute, they turned in unison, seeming surprised by the sound of hooves.

"Rachel!" Lovina cried, waving.

Daniel slowed the cart and Rachel forced a smile onto her face.

"*Moin*," she greeted the couple, willing tears not to well in her eyes.

"Come with us for a walk," Lovina implored. "We are headed to the lake."

"I can't," Rachel responded, a sudden resolve growing inside her. "I must pack."

Lovina stared at her uncomprehendingly.

"Pack?" she echoed, glancing at Jacob who seemed equally confused and Rachel nodded.

"Yes," Rachel said firmly. "I am leaving for Holmesville this weekend."

And as she said it, studying her best friend's face register shock, Rachel suddenly was sure she was doing the right thing.

If I am made to stay here and see their happiness while my heart breaks, I will go mad.

"Okay boys and girls, settle down," Mrs. Verhoot instructed, clapping her hands together. "We have a new teacher today."

The unruly mass of children blatantly ignored the older woman and continued to yell and squabble amongst themselves.

Mrs. Verhoot tried again.

"Children!" she called, thumping her coffee mug against the table. "Attention please!"

A few eyes trained toward the front and suddenly one girl tittered as she saw Rachel. She pointed and whispered to her friend who turned to spread the secret to the next group.

Soon, the class was silent but for a sprinkling of giggles as the children stared at her.

"Take your seats, children," Mrs. Verhoot instructed, seeming relieved that they were finally listening. "Everyone, this is Miss Littwiller."

The quiet sniggering became blatant laughter.

Rachel turned to her co-worker in confusion.

"Quiet down now!" Mrs. Verhoot growled. "Miss Littwiller – "

The chortles grew louder, and Rachel's eyebrows knit in confusion.

"Why are the chuckling?" she asked Mrs. Verhoot, not understanding the joke but the older woman did not answer, scowling at the class.

"That is enough!" she cried, her face growing red. "Miss Littwiller is your elder and commands your respect. She is here to help with your studies. Am I understood."

They tried to contain themselves, but the smirks did not disappear from their collective faces and Rachel could feel her ears growing red with humiliation.

She knew they were laughing at her, but she could not say why.

As the day progressed, she heard them tittering about her name and her clothes and as lunchtime came, Rachel was sure she was crimson with embarrassment.

She gathered her lunch from the staff room and looked around for a place to eat in peace.

There were several tables already occupied by staff, but no one offered her a place at theirs and Rachel was too shy to ask for a seat.

In fact, the other teachers seemed determined to avoid eye contact with Rachel, deliberately turning their shoulders away from her as if to discourage her from approaching.

You are imagining things, she told herself. *Those children have made you irrational.*

Still, Rachel did not take the chance that they would reject her.

Instead, she took her bag and wandered out of the room toward the playing field in search of sanctuary.

Her long skirt swirled around her ankles and she finally found a quiet spot near the edge of the property beneath a giant oak.

Tucking her legs beneath her, Rachel flipped her long braid over her shoulder and reached inside the lunch bag for some bread and cheese.

She had not had much of an opportunity to do shopping since moving into her small apartment on Taylor Street, but she had not realized how hungry she would find herself by lunchtime.

Tomorrow I will pack a heftier lunch, she told herself. *Who would have thought that this job would be so tiring?*

Rachel tried not to think about the impending hours.

"Are you Miss Littwiller?"

She gazed up at the speaker, a tall, thin man in his early thirties in a Polo shirt and loose-fitting jeans.

He was handsome in an academic way, wire rim glasses hiding long lashed blue eyes.

"Yes," she replied.

He presented her with a quick smile and even in its fleetingness, Rachel noticed how white were his teeth.

"Principal Cotton is looking for you," he said. "They made an announcement in the school on the public announcement system, but I suppose you didn't hear it all the way out here."

Rachel rose, shaking her head so her prayer cap strings slapped her mouth gently.

"Thank you," she said, gathering her scraps of food and packing them back in the bag.

He watched her with curious eyes and Rachel felt a slow blush creep up her neck.

"Is there something else?" she asked, and he seemed surprised to find he was still staring at her.

Quickly he shook his head.

"Uh...no...I'm David Mathers, by the way."

She didn't respond, hurrying back toward the school and through the corridors.

That was very rude of you, Rachel reproached herself. *He is the only person who has reached out to you since you've been here, and you did not even introduce yourself properly.*

Rachel knew it had nothing to do with the kind stranger and more to do with her nerves. She wondered what Principal Cotton wanted with her now.

Have I done something already? I have only been here for four hours!

It seemed suddenly as if everyone was staring at her whereas earlier, she could not catch one person's attention.

Inside the office, Amy leered at her from the desk, causing Rachel's anxiety to mount.

"Go right in, Rachel," she instructed in a smug tone. "Principal Cotton is waiting for you although he did call for you ten minutes ago."

Rachel did as she was told, rapping on the inner door gently.

"I said go in!" Amy snapped. "Can't you follow simple instructions?"

Again, Rachel ignored the receptionist and waited for Principal Cotton to acknowledge her.

"Come in, Rachel," he called, and she noticed that his tone was much less friendly than it had been the first time they had met.

"You wanted to see me, Principal Cotton?" she asked tentatively as she entered.

He glanced up from his computer screen, his jaw tightening slightly as he saw her.

A chubby hand waved her further inside.

"Please sit down. I feel like we had a miscommunication when I hired you," he started. "But there are some things we need to discuss immediately, some concerns I have."

Rachel felt her back grow rigid and she chewed on her lower lip.

I have done something wrong!

"Such as?" she choked, wracking her brain to think of what it was.

Principal Cotton cleared his throat and shifted his eyes downward.

"For example, your attire. Now I realize that you come from a simple lifestyle, but the parents of the students expect a certain decorum from the teachers. We cannot have you dressed so..."

He trailed off and Rachel tried not to gape.

Principal Cotton cleared his throat and seemed to balk at Rachel's open-mouthed stare.

"You understand I mean no offense, Rachel," he told her. "I am only explaining to you the requirements of the job."

"I see," she mumbled. "Anything else?"

His porcine eyes darted around the room again before resting on her face.

"Perhaps we should shorten your name to Miss L. It will be easier and less distracting for the children to absorb."

Suddenly, it made sense; the whispers and mocking.

I am expected to appease the children when they are acting cruelly? What kind of adults will they grow up to be if not taught to respect their elders? She wondered.

Rachel's stomach seemed to flip as she gazed at her boss, unsure of how to react.

One part of her wanted to run from the office and forget she had ever decided to take such a wretched position but when she thought of Jacob and Lovina walking arm in arm near her home, there was only one option.

"Rachel, please don't look so devastated," Principal Cotton pleaded. "These changes are as much for your benefit as they are everyone else's. If you give these parents and kids things to take issue with, they will come at you mercilessly. I am only trying to make the transition easier for you."

Rachel swallowed thickly and nodded.

"I understand," she whispered, casting her eyes toward her hands. "I will ensure I am better dressed tomorrow."

The principal cleared his throat and shook his head.

"I was thinking you could go shopping now," he told her. "Take the afternoon to do that and start fresh again tomorrow. We'll pretend today never happened."

As if it would be so simple to forget about today, Rachel thought miserably.

There was no room for argument in his tone and she bobbed her head stiffly.

"As you wish," she replied quietly, rising from the edge of the chair.

They did not exchange another word as Rachel left the office, avoiding Amy's smirk. As she ventured out of the office, she heard the mean-spirited woman speak loudly.

The conversation was meant to be between herself and Principal Cotton, but Rachel could tell Amy wanted her to hear.

"That's what you get for hiring a child with Grade Eight education!" Amy snickered. "What were you thinking, Charles?"

Rachel paused to hear the older man's response.

"What choice did I have, Amy? It's not like we are teeming with applicants out here in Holmesville. She will do – for now. It's in her contract. We can replace her on a whim if someone better comes along."

Shock filled Rachel's body and she ran from the school, her hands trembling.

She had disappointed her parents, uprooted her life in the district and walked into something far worse.

Or was it?

Once more, the image of Lovina and Jacob's wedding filled her mind and Rachel was sure that nothing would be more torturous than returning home to see that.

You must give this life a chance, she tried to reassure herself. *As Principal Cotton said, this is an adjustment for everyone. I cannot make an informed decision after one day.*

Yet as she made her way into the center of town, searching for a decent place to buy Englisch clothes, Rachel wondered if she would ever belong anywhere ever again.

The following day, Rachel was at school before anyone else.

She nodded at the janitor as she made her way into Mrs. Verhoot's classroom, determined to have a better day.

The previous night, she had stayed awake, thinking of ways to win over her co-workers and the children.

She was feeling confident when she finally fell asleep at three o'clock in the morning but in the light of day, she was no longer certain she knew what she was doing.

You will be a wonderful teacher, she promised herself. *No matter what Principal Cotton and Amy think of your. You will make yourself indispensable to the school and they will not even consider another for your position.*

As she sat at the desk, writing down her ideas for Mrs. Verhoot, she suddenly got the sense that she was being watched.

Rachel's head bolted up and she gasped slightly as she recognized the man in the doorway.

"Uh, hey," he said. "Sorry, you just looked so lost in thought there and I didn't want to interrupt you."

She simply stared at him in confusion.

His brown eyebrows made a vee and he walked toward her.

"I'm David Mathers. I teach Fourth Grade – we met yesterday on the field," he explained, and she nodded quickly.

"Yes, of course," she replied. "Rachel Littwiller. I...I'm sorry if I was rude yesterday."

He shook his head.

"I understand you're having a classic Thomas Jefferson start here," he replied dryly. "Don't apologize to me. I'm sorry this place is so wretched to newcomers."

He offered his hand and she accepted it briefly before darting her eyes back toward the page before her.

"You look much different out of your dress," David said and his face blushed scarlet. "I mean, you look different wearing slacks."

Rachel swallowed a smile, shaking her head.

It felt odd not wearing her prayer cap, but she did not know if it was permitted and she didn't want to be called back into Principal Cotton's office.

"I did not realize there was a dress requirement before I started," Rachel explained, her face turning pink at the memory of being called to the office.

David seemed annoyed.

"There are several things about this school which are unfair and unnecessary," he replied curtly, and Rachel glanced up at him in surprise. There was a slight anger in his voice but before she could ask him anything further, Mrs. Verhoot appeared at the doorway.

"Oh! Don't you look nice, dear!" the woman cried, clapping her hands together in her regular dramatic fashion. "Doesn't she look nice, Mr. Mathers?"

David shrugged and turned to leave.

"I think she looks uncomfortable being forced to wear something she doesn't want to wear," he replied but he was gone before anyone could respond.

Rachel felt a spark of hope in her heart as he left.

He was the first person she had met outside the district who didn't seem to dislike her.

Perhaps there was hope for her in the Englisch world after all.

The small feeling of victory did not last however, and by day's end, Rachel's nerves were frazzled.

The children seemed determined to make her life unmanageable, misbehaving, throwing things and getting into trouble.

Mrs. Verhoot had dismissed her recommendations, making Rachel feel like an incompetent fool as she condescendingly explained why her ideas would not work.

At lunch she still could not find anyone with whom to speak and she found herself looking for David, but he was not in the staffroom.

She considered asking someone where to find him, but she worried how that would be perceived when she was already under such fine scrutiny.

She did not see the Fourth-Grade teacher for the rest of the day and when Rachel finally found herself at the low-rise apartment building, she was looking forward to a bath and reading a book.

What she had not expected was seeing her mother waiting for her in the lobby, seeming out of place and uncomfortable.

"*Mammi!*" Rachel cried, hurrying to embrace her mother. "What are you doing here? Is it *Daed*? Leah?"

Ruth shook her graying head, eyeing her daughter's outfit. Rachel could see she was desperately trying not to pass judgement with her eyes.

"No, liebchen. Everyone is fine," Ruth replied. "I have come to see your apartment."

Rachel gave her a sidelong look.

"All right," she said slowly and leading the way to her ground floor unit. "Are you certain everyone is well?"

Ruth nodded quickly, and Rachel sighed in relief.

She is worried about me, she realized. *A mother always knows when her child needs her.*

"Would you like some tea, *Mammi*?" Rachel asked as they entered the small apartment.

"No, Rachel, I would like for you to come home now."

The words were not surprising, but they caught Rachel off guard nonetheless.

She exhaled heavily and faced her mother.

"Mammi, I cannot simply leave the job I just started," she told Ruth. "I have a contract, an obligation."

"You have an obligation to your community too, Rachel," her mother reminded her, and the younger woman cringed.

"*Mammi,* please, you must understand – "

"No, I do not understand but if this is truly what you want, I cannot stop you and I will always love you. That said…"

Ruth trailed off and grasped Rachel's hands.

"Gideon Smith has been asking about you since you left. He was gravely disappointed to hear you had taken this job."

Rachel cocked her head to the side and studied her mother's face.

"Really?" she asked.

Rachel was not sure what to do with that information.

Gideon was an older man, widowed with a young daughter whom Rachel cared for a great deal. But to consider Gideon a suitor? Never. Rachel's dreams had always included Jacob.

But now Jacob is spoken for. And you are alone in a world where you are disrespected and demeaned. Gideon Smith would make a decent husband.

"Perhaps you should consider your options for marriage, Rachel," Ruth said softly. "I see you are thinking about it."

Rachel knew she would never feel toward Gideon as she did Jacob.

But it was still the prospect of marriage.

You vowed to give this job a chance, she reminded herself. *You have not even given it two full days. And what kind of marriage would it be to Gideon? A marriage to a man you do not love while you see the one you do with someone else.*

Rachel shook her head.

"No, *Mammi,*" she said firmly. "I must complete my contract with the school. Perhaps later I can think about coming home."

Ruth's mouth became a fine line of anger, but she did not argue.

"Your father warned me not to come. He thought that you would say such a thing, but I wanted you to know that you are not forgotten in the district."

Rachel nodded slowly.

"*Danke, Mammi,*" she said earnestly. "I needed to hear that."

Mother and daughter locked gazes and Ruth touched her cheek gently.

"Everything will work out the way *Gotte* intends, *liebchen,*" Ruth told her. "You must trust in His will."

Rachel hoped her mother was right.

As the second progressed, Rachel found herself thinking of Gideon Smith more often.

She asked herself if she was being unreasonable by dismissing him so easily.

After all, she did adore his daughter, Ivy and he was a kind man from the little she knew of him. It was slightly startling to learn that he had affections for her.

I imagine that Jacob would be stunned to learn I had feelings for him also, she mused and in the end, it always circled back to Lovina and Jacob.

By Friday afternoon, Rachel decided she would return to the district and visit her family.

She missed her parents and sister terribly, but she was plagued by the fear of seeing her best friend with Jacob.

Surely it must get easier, Rachel thought as she packed up her attaché case and looked around to ensure she had not forgotten anything.

A quiet knock on the door caught her attention and she turned to see David Mathers in the doorway.

"You made it through your first two weeks," he told her, grinning. "And you are still standing!"

She smiled and nodded.

"I suppose that is something to be grateful for," she agreed.

"How are the kids treating you?" David asked, and Rachel peered at him for a long moment without speaking.

Slowly, his beam faded.

"Uh oh," he commented. "That badly?"

Rachel shook her head.

"No," she answered as if suddenly realizing that the children had not been as mischievous the past day or so. "They have been quite good, in fact."

David's face brightened.

"Well that's good," he remarked. "I knew it would just be a matter of time before you found your groove. What about the staff?"

Rachel laughed.

"Well you have been very kind to me, but I believe everyone else thinks I have no right to be here."

David frowned.

"It doesn't matter what anyone else thinks," he growled in annoyance. "You are doing a wonderful job reaching the children. I wish the adults would act with some maturity too."

Rachel was slightly taken aback by his outburst.

"You do not think highly of the teachers?"

David shrugged, trying to appear nonchalant but Rachel could read the irritation in his eyes.

"It is not that they are bad teachers, but they act like small children themselves. They have their own tables in the breakroom and gossip about one another. It is just like being in high school," he grumbled. "I think it has much to do with the small-town mentality. In city schools, the teachers are not so childish."

Rachel's eyebrows shot up.

"You have taught in city schools?"

"I used to teach in Columbus before I got transferred here. I have put out my resume to get in a school in Akron but who knows if a position will come available."

An unexpected pang shot through Rachel.

You can't leave me here! I have no other friends if you go! She wanted to yell but she held her reaction and smiled weakly.

"Well I am certain that you will do very well no matter where you go," she told him. He returned her beam and a short pause fell between them.

"So...uh, do you have plans for the weekend, Rachel?" he asked.

"I am going home to visit my family," she told him. "There is no service on Sunday this week, so I will have an extra day with my parents and sister."

David nodded.

"That sounds good."

They gazed at one another somewhat awkwardly and Rachel gestured at her bag.

"I should be going," she said. "I will see you Monday."

David nodded.

"If I haven't moved to Akron," he joked but the words sent another shiver of panic through Rachel.

What if he really does go to Akron? She wondered as she left the school.

She didn't want to think about it.

"You have come home!" Ruth gasped as Rachel walked inside the house.

"Just for a visit, *Mammi*," Rachel replied quickly, careful not to raise her mother's hopes unrealistically.

"We are happy to have you, *liebchen* but you should have told us you were coming," Daniel chided. "We people coming for supper tonight and you will be riddled with questions."

Rachel grimaced at the thought.

All week she had been at the mercy of strangers. The last thing she wanted was to endure the same treatment with those she loved.

"I should not have come," Rachel sighed, turning back toward the door.

"Do not be foolish!" Leah called, racing down the stairs. "We will be amongst friends tonight. *Daed*, you should not have made her feel shamed for returning home."

Ruth and Leah glared at Daniel and he looked at Rachel with contrition.

"Of course she should not feel shamed," he exclaimed. "You are always welcome home, *Lieb*. Come out of the doorway now and put your bag in your bedroom."

Rachel felt torn, glancing helplessly at her sister who ushered her onto the second floor.

"How is it living among the Englisch?" Leah demanded. "Tell me about your apartment!"

Rachel glanced at her sixteen-year-old sister who had not yet experienced Rumspringa and she tried to remember if she had ever been so fascinated with Englisch culture.

I never wanted to leave the community, Rachel thought and even when Lovina and the others were wearing Englisch clothes or smoking cigarettes, Rachel had known her place was in the district.

Yet at that moment, Rachel wanted to retreat back to her apartment in Holmesville.

The conflict inside her was real and while she was happy to see her family, Rachel could not stop comparing the luxuries she had inside her one-bedroom unit to the simple ways of the farmhouse.

"Rachel? Are you all right?" Leah asked, and the older sister forced a smile.

"Yes. You must come and visit me," she said, shifting her thoughts away from her new life.

"Will you come home and marry Gideon Smith?" Leah asked, and Rachel's green eyes widened in shock.

"Did *Mammi* tell you that?" she demanded. Leah nodded.

"I said no such thing," Rachel muttered. "No, I will not marry Gideon Smith."

"Who will you marry then?"

Rachel stared at her for a long moment.

"Maybe an Englischer," she replied haughtily, and Leah gasped.

"You are not coming back, Rachel?" she demanded. "But *Mammi* said – "

"What *Mammi* hopes and what is real are two different things," Rachel interrupted. "I have a job now at the school and perhaps it could be a career for me."

"You like it so much?" Leah asked, and Rachel cringed inwardly.

I cannot lie to her.

"Leah! Rachel! Our guests have arrived!" Ruth called from the downstairs landing.

"Come along," Rachel said, and Leah grabbed her arm.

"You cannot go like that," she breathed.

Rachel gazed down at her pantsuit and sighed.

She had forgotten what she was wearing.

"I will change and be down in a moment," she said.

As Leah left the room, Rachel peered down at her outfit once more.

She couldn't recall the moment when the clothes had become comfortable. It seemed that one day she had felt terribly uncomfortable in such foreign garments and the next they had become second skin.

Slowly, she put on a homemade brown dress and brushed her tresses away from her face.

As she peered at herself in the mirror, another obscure thought popped into her head.

I should see about acquiring a haircut.

"Rachel!"

"Coming *Mamm*!" she called back, whirling away from the mirror. She hurried down the stairs toward the sitting room where she froze in her tracks.

"Rachel! You have come home!" Lovina squealed happily, hurrying to embrace her. "Why didn't you tell us you were coming?"

She disentangled herself from Lovina arms and smiled at her friend's parents.

"I wanted it to be a surprise."

Jacob also grinned from the corner where he sat with his brothers and father.

"*Moin*, Rachel!" he called disarmingly.

Rachel stared at him, her mind beginning to turn.

For the first time since they had announced their engagement, she did not feel an overwhelming sense of heartbreak.

A small twinge affected her heartbeat, but it was nothing compared to the agony she had felt before.

"*Moin*, Jacob," she replied easily, and the words did not stick in her throat.

It is getting better! Rachel thought, a deep breath of relief passing through her.

As they gathered around to dinner, Rachel wondered what had changed.

She no longer found herself pining after Jacob or envying Lovina. Instead her mind was somewhere else, in a classroom, picking up her books at the end of the day.

She was not playing the "what if" game but glancing over at the threshold where David Mathers was waiting for her.

Nothing has changed except for me, she realized. *I am moving onward with my life.*

A sudden elation filled Rachel and she knew then what she had to do.

"Good morning, David," she called, and he started as he flicked on the light of his classroom.

"Rachel!" he gasped. "You surprised me. Why are you sitting in the dark?"

"It isn't dark," she laughed. "And I am Amish. I am used to much less lighting than this."

David chuckled and dropped his books on the desk in front of her.

"Did you have a good weekend?" he asked, and she nodded.

"I did. And you?"

David shrugged.

"It was not very eventful, but my weekends never are," he replied. "What are you doing here?"

"I came to ask you something," Rachel answered, slipping off his chair.

"Ask away."

"I wanted to know if you would eat lunch with me today."

His eyebrows shot up in shock.

"Really?" he laughed. "Are you asking me to your table?"

Rachel nodded.

"I thought we could start our own table. There is no need for us to be isolated while the others sit together."

His face lit up completely.

"I would like that," he replied.

Rachel steadied her trembling hands and nodded.

"Are you okay, Rachel?" David asked gently, and she bobbed her head enthusiastically.

"I think so," she told him, and she meant it.

She didn't know where things would go with David or if they would go anywhere at all, but Rachel did know that each day she spent among the Englisch taught her more about herself and that was not something she was going to give up on, especially not when she had an ally on her side.

While she loved her family and her community, Rachel was in no rush to return, not until she had fully experienced what she was just getting a taste of; her independence.

"Why are you staring at me like that?" David asked.

"Tell me more about Akron," she said.

LOVINA'S HEART

DEIDRA SCOTT

Chapter One

Lovina Miller took a deep breath as she reached up to pull a piece of laundry from the clothesline and put it in the basket at her feet. Above her head, a pair of bluebirds danced through the bright June sky, reminding her that summer was quickly approaching.

Summer. It was a time full of fresh starts and new beginnings.

Looking across the yard, Lovina watched David Yoder working with one of her brothers. Together, the two young men were struggling with their task, trying to break her *daed's* new horse.

Ach, just watching David sent a thrill of excitement through Lovina's heart. Although she had known him most of her life, there was something about him that could still put a spark inside of her, giving her the feeling that they had just met.

Growing up, Lovina had always dreamed of marrying David. It had just seemed natural to her. With their two houses located side-by-side, they had spent all of their childhood hours playing together in the creek that wound between their properties and climbing the big apple tree like little monkeys.

Lovina had decided early on that she and David would grow old together, spending their adult days raising babies and making a life within their Amish community.

Now that Lovina had turned eighteen-years-old, she felt like she was stuck in the midst of a waiting game, simply counting down the hours until David came forward to begin their relationship together.

Smiling to herself, Lovina basked in the realization that, as an adult, it was now time to watch her childhood dreams start to unfold.

"*Danki* for the help, David!" Lovina heard her father call out from the barn and looked up in time to see David waving goodbye to her family as he started across the yard.

Lovina felt her heart go aflutter when, rather than take the path back to his own parents' house, David veered closer to her own home and made a bee-line right for the clothesline where she was working.

"*Gut* afternoon, David!" Lovina called out, her voice seeming somewhat weak to her own ears.

Watching him come closer, Lovina couldn't help but marvel at how handsome her childhood friend had become. With a head-full of dark red hair and sparkling blue eyes, David had always looked like a cheerful storybook character; however, as he aged, he grew tall and muscular, his boyish looks transforming into that of a good-looking man.

"Hello there, Lovina," David called back, rolling down his sleeves as he walked along, "I tell you, that horse of your *daed's* nearly got me down this time!"

Lovina smiled as she pulled a pair of her brother's pants off of the laundry line and tossed them in the basket, "I guess we should consider ourselves glad to have such a good horse-breaker living so near-by."

To her surprise, David's face suddenly seemed to darken. Taking a deep breath, he reached up and put one hand on the clothesline, "Actually, Lovina, I wanted to talk to you about that."

Although Lovina had hoped that David would want to talk to her alone, she could already tell that his news wasn't going to be what she had wanted to hear.

"Lovina," David looked out across the fields, "Ever since you had your birthday, I'd been hoping..." his voice trailed off and he gave a shrug, "Well, nothing I'd hoped for is going to work out this summer." Standing up taller, he announced, "My uncle from Indiana wrote telling about the need for a good horse-trainer in his community. I agreed to go help for the next three months...I'll be home in time to help my dad get started on the harvest."

Lovina felt her heart drop in her chest. The idea that David would leave had never entered her mind. Even though it was only for three months, it felt like it might as well be three years.

"*Ach*, Lovina, don't be so sad," David reached out and placed his hand on her arm, "I'll be back – I promise. Kentucky is my home...I sure don't have any plans to run off for good."

Something about having his hand on her arm made the pain a little more bearable. Looking up, Lovina met David's tender gaze with her own.

"When I come back..." David took a deep breath and kicked at a clump of grass with his foot. It was strange to see him so uncomfortable – David was usually one to be bold and daring, willing to say whatever was necessary.

"When I come back, I hope we can spend more time together," David managed to say, "Seems like we've grown apart over the years, and I'm ready for that to end."

Lovina couldn't stop the smile that spread across her face, "And maybe not be climbing trees this time?" She added.

David laughed, "Of course we'll be climbing trees again!" He teased.

Growing more sober, he lifted his hand and ran it gently across her cheek, "I'll see you in three months, 'Vina."

Three months. As she watched him walk away and back to his parents' farm across the creek, Lovina took a deep breath and tried to still her thumping heart. Three months was a long time – she was just glad that she had those tender moments to cling to during the summer that stretched out before her.

Chapter Two

Taking a deep breath, David watched out the passenger window as the driver he had hired took him farther and farther from his home in Kentucky and on toward his Uncle Amos' house in Indiana.

"Are you nervous about leaving home for so long?" David's paid driver, Mr. Simpson asked, as he flipped his turn signal on and proceeded toward Uncle Amos' house.

David shook his head and laughed, "*Ach*, no, not nervous."

"Anxious to get away from your parents?" Mr. Simpson asked with a chuckle.

"No, nothing like that." David assured him, "Just glad to be helping my uncle and the people in his community."

Leaning his head back against the headrest of the seat, David closed his eyes and thought about Mr. Simpson's question.

Was he glad to be getting away from his parents? Although he had been quick to assure his driver that wasn't he case, David wasn't so certain himself. To be completely honest, David wasn't a bit sorry to be leaving for the summer. While he had always loved his home and his family, David relished the chance to get away.

Since David had been a little boy, he had always known what was expected of him. He was going to settle down, buy a piece of property close to his parents, and marry Lovina Miller. It wasn't a bad plan at all, but it seemed so boring and dull. Deep in his heart, David had always dreamed of excitement and adventure. Maybe his trip to Indiana would finally provide him with a chance to enjoy his freedom before he settled down for good.

David's driver took him straight to Uncle Amos' house, helped him unload his bags, and then left him to head back to Kentucky.

Uncle Amos and his entire family were happy to welcome David to their home. Uncle Amos explained that everyone in the community could use his horse breaking services and that they would be bringing their horses to his house so that David could train them. Uncle Amos also said that, during David's spare time he could help the family out in the dry goods store they had located in a small shed next to the road.

"I'll take you out to the store now, so that I can show you what kind of work you can do out there." Uncle Amos suggested once David had put his clothes away in the spare bedroom.

Leading David across the yard, Uncle Amos explained, "Of course, I will pay you for helping in the store...and you can also have all the money for training the horses."

David shook his head, "*Ach,* that's too much, Uncle Amos. I'm happy to have the chance to help out."

Uncle Amos chuckled and reached out to give David a slap on the back, "Now, now, don't go talking like that. I'm sure a handsome young man like you should be saving back to buy a nice farm and making plans for the future. I'd dare say that some pretty girl back home has caught your eye."

David gave a shrug, not too anxious to think about his future, "Nothing set in stone just yet."

The graveled lane ended and the two men found themselves standing side-by-side outside of the dry goods store. Reaching out, Uncle Amos pushed the door open, revealing a building with shelves full of baking supplies, canned goods, and some craft items.

"Hannah!" Uncle Amos called out, as he led David through the small building, "Hannah!"

"I'm over here," a soft voice returned.

Turning the corner around one of the shelves, they found a young Amish woman on her knees, busy stacking bags of flour.

"Hannah, I want you to meet my nephew, David," Uncle Amos announced, "David, this is Hannah – she is my wife's cousin and she's helping us out in the store this summer."

Hannah pulled herself to her feet and turned to stare up at David with large, blue eyes. Wisps of dark hair had escaped her prayer *kapp*, making a sort of halo around her face.

Just looking at her, David felt his heart give a leap. She was so unexpectedly beautiful in a dark, mysterious way.

"*Gut* to meet you, David," Hannah replied timidly.

"David is likely to be helping out in the store when he isn't working with the horses," Uncle Amos explained. Giving David a pat on the arm, he motioned toward the back room, "Come on, I want to show you where I store the bulk supplies."

As David followed his uncle, he had a hard time even listening to what was being said. His mind was still mesmerized by the beautiful and timid young lady he had just met. David could hardly wait to get to know and learn more about Hannah.

Lovina sat on the edge of her bed, looking out across the fields of farmland through her bedroom window. Knowing that David was no longer in the house next-door left a hollow emptiness in Lovina's heart. In her eighteen-years, she had never gone a summer without seeing David.

Lovina tired to imagine what her sweet friend was doing at that moment. Did he realize how much she was thinking of him? Did he miss her at all?

Lovina closed her eyes and took a deep breath, "Dear God," she whispered into the darkness, "Please, bring the man that I love back to me."

Chapter Three

David carefully guided his uncle's buggy down the road. It was only his second day in Indiana and work was already starting to pick up; however, Uncle Amos had sent him to town to pick up some nails for a woodworking project he was doing in the barn.

The summer afternoon sun shone down on David and the warmth of the breeze put a smile on his face. David was enjoying his time away from home and, although he had not had many opportunities to spend time with Hannah, he had hopes that would change eventually.

The buggy suddenly took a lung, pulling David out of his thoughts.

"Woah, boy! Woah!" David pulled tightly on the reigns, unsure of what was happening to the buggy. Carefully guiding the horse to the side of the road, he jumped down from his seat and looked over the situation.

Something was wrong with the front buggy wheel. Grabbing a hold of it, David gave it a wiggle, trying to determine if it could keep going.

Pulling off his straw hat, David slapped it against his leg in frustration. He couldn't get to town on that wheel and he didn't think he could make it back to his uncle's house either.

The clipping of oncoming horse hooves made David stand up straighter and wave desperately at the approaching buggy.

The driver was a single Amish man. As soon as David caught his attention, the other driver pulled his buggy to the side of the road behind David.

"Hi there!" David greeted with a smile as he watched the other Amish man get off his buggy and start toward him, "Boy, I sure am glad to see you!" Sticking out a hand, he announced, "I'm David Yoder. I'm staying with my Uncle Amos Yoder – you probably know him."

The stranger nodded and simply said, "I'm Luke Christner." Taking a deep breath, he walked over to the buggy and squatted down to inspect the wheel.

"Looks like this is busted good," he announced, pushing his hat back on his head and reaching up to wipe some sweat from his brow.

David groaned, "I was afraid of that."

Standing to his feet, Luke continued, "I'm afraid you shouldn't drive it any farther than just a few feet or you'll end up wrecking or destroying your entire buggy." With a slight smirk, Luke added, "Lucky for you, this is my parents' drive right up ahead. And I just happen to work on buggies for a living."

David's eyes got large and he let out a huge sigh, "Oh, *gut*! Do you think that you could help me out?"

Luke nodded, "Sure thing. Just lead your buggy down to my workshop. I'll have her fixed up in just a bit."

True to his word, Luke had the buggy wheel fixed within an hour.

David stayed by the young man who had rescued him and worked to fill him in on all the details about his life, his home, and his family. Luke, who seemed to be more reserved, was happy to listen and donate very few details of his own.

"How much do I owe you?" David asked as Luke put the repaired wheel back on his buggy.

Luke gave a shrug as he secured the wheel in place, "Nothing. Consider it a welcome present. Maybe you can help me with one of my horses one day this summer."

"*Ach*," David raised an eyebrow, "I can't let you do that. I took some time you could have been working on other projects…"

Before he could finished, Luke started shaking his head, "No, no you didn't," he assured David as he stood up straight, "Honestly, I didn't have any other work for today." Sighing deeply, he announced, "As badly as we need a horse trainer in this area, we do not need any kind of buggy work. Jobs around here are scarce, David. I was glad to help."

David pondered Luke's statement for a moment. As an idea entered his mind, a broad smile spread across his face, "Listen, Luke! You may not be needed here, but you sure would be in my community! How would you feel about going to Kentucky to spend the summer with my family? It would sure help them out while I'm gone, and you could earn money doing buggy repairs and carpentry work!"

Luke was silent, obviously studying David's suggestion. Finally, with a shrug, he announced, "*Jah* – I don't see why that wouldn't be great. *Danki*, David."

The entire plan made David's face light up like that of a little boy. Grinning from ear-to-ear, he grabbed his new friend's hand in a shake and started making plans to get Luke back to Kentucky.

Chapter Four

Lovina reached up to wipe some sweat from her forehead as she took a break from chopping weeds out of the row of green beans. Despite all her hard work, the weeds were quickly starting to overtake the plants.

David had now been gone two weeks, and Lovina had yet to hear anything from him. His absence made her sad and she wished for all she was worth that she would receive a letter.

Glancing across the field toward his house, she thought of all the times they had snuck away from their chores and played together instead.

To her surprise, Lovina saw a young man approaching her. Could it be...? Lovina's heart dropped as he drew closer. Although she had hoped that it was David, she instantly realized that her eyes had been playing tricks on her. This stranger was even taller than her dear childhood friend and slightly thinner.

"Hullo," Lovina called out as he continued to draw closer.

"Hullo," the stranger returned, his voice deep and almost mysterious, "Are you Lovina Miller?"

Lovina stood up straighter and adjusted her prayer *kapp*, "That would be me. Do I know you?"

The stranger shook his head, "No, you don't." Now he was so close that Lovina was able to get a good look at him. This strange Amish man looked to be in his early twenties, but he seemed more mature. His brown hair was so dark it was almost black, and his eyes a dark color chocolate. Just looking at him made Lovina take a deep breath of surprise. *Ach*, it was hard to remember a time that she had ever seen such a *gut*-looking man!

"I'm Luke Christner. I know your friend, David, and I'm staying with his family until he returns." Glancing toward her house, Luke asked, "Is your *daed* at home? The Yoders told me that he has a construction crew and I'd like a job."

Lovina felt so out of sorts, she wasn't sure what to do. Looking down at her bare feet, she tried to gather her composure. Taking a deep breath, she said, "*Nee*, my *daed* isn't home from work yet, but we're expecting him any minute. If you'd like to wait in the house, my *mamm* can give you some fresh lemonade and cookies."

Luke glanced from the house back to Lovina and then shrugged, "If you don't mind, I'll just stay out here. Looks like you could use some help." Grabbing for an extra hoe, Luke set to work, removing the pesky weeds from among the rows of bean plants.

There was something about Luke that made Lovina feel uncertain about everything. He was a good help in the garden, but she certainly would have felt more at-ease without him. On the other hand, she dreaded him leaving once her father got home from work. Just being near him made her feel things that she had never experienced – she found herself overwhelmed by a sort of giddiness that sprung up from deep within. Although Lovina had always been a talker, she suddenly seemed almost speechless.

"You don't have to do this," Lovina assured him.

Luke simply set his jaw and turned to look at her with his brooding, dark eyes, "I don't have to...but I want to."

Lovina felt weak in the knees, as if she might keel right over. Taking a deep breath, she tried to stead herself.

Suddenly, she found herself a little glad that David was going to be gone for the summer. As quickly as the thought flitted through her mind, she pushed it away; however, just the realization that she could think such a thing left Lovina questioning everything about the future.

David washed his hands in a pail of water that had been set out by the barn, preparing himself for the evening meal. Inside the house, Aunt Miriam was putting the finishing touches on a pot of homemade chili with the help of three of David's cousins.

True to Uncle Amos' word, in the time that David had spent in Indiana he had already been so busy, he hardly had time to even think about being at home.

Wiping his clean hands on a towel, David glanced across the acres of land that his uncle owned. There, in the glowing darkness of the evening, he could make out the form of a young woman walking near the pond.

Hannah.

David had learned to recognize her from a distance. Even though it would be hard to distinguish her from any other Amish woman from so far away, David could pick Hannah out because she was always alone. It seemed like she carried an air of sadness with her, wherever she went.

Taking a deep breath, David stepped out of the barn and started the short walk to the pond.

"Hi there," David called out as he drew near to Hannah.

The young woman looked up at him and gave a sad smile.

"What are you doing?"

Hannah gave a shrug and pulled her black shawl tighter against her shoulders, "I just felt like a walk," she explained.

David stepped up next to her side, "It must be sort of lonely to walk all alone."

Hannah shrugged again, "I'm used to being alone."

David *thought* over his childhood and how little time he had ever spent just to himself. There were always siblings to play with, other Amish children to enjoy at events, and Lovina. Lovina had always been there for him.

Just the thought of his old friend's name sent a nagging sense of guilt through his mind.

Hadn't he promised Lovina that, when he got home, things would be different? Hadn't he promised that they would spend time together? So, what was he doing, trying to get closer to Hannah?

"David..." Hannah's soft voice brought him out of his thoughts, "Are you all right, David? I've never seen you so solemn and quiet."

David looked up at her in surprise, his face breaking out in a broad grin, "Oh, *jah*, I'm fine. I was just thinking is all."

"I didn't know you were able to do that...you know, think without saying what was going through your mind." Although Hannah's words were haughty, David *looked* up in time to catch a teasing smile cross her lips. It was the first time he had ever seen her smile and, something about it made him want to see it a thousand times more.

"Maybe it's too much time around you," David suggested, "Because I don't think you ever say anything much at all."

Hannah's tender smirk turned into a broad smile and David was, once again, captivated by her charm.

Reaching out, he gently took her elbow in his hand, "Would you do me the honor of letting me walk with ya tonight?"

Hannah was silent for a moment, studying David for all that he was worth. Finally, she nodded slowly and said, "*Jah* – I suppose that might be nice."

Chapter Five

Just as David had predicted, it was easy for Luke to find work in Kentucky. He not only spent his afternoons working on buggies in the Yoder's empty shed, but also joined the carpentry work crew lead by Lovina's father.

Lovina wasn't exactly sure how it happened, but it seemed that she and Luke were constantly thrown in the paths of one another. Lovina tried to convince herself that it was merely a coincidence, but she had to admit that it was more than that.

The longer David was gone, the less she was thinking about him and the more she was thinking about Luke.

When he wasn't busy with work, Luke frequently dropped by to help Lovina in the garden; although he wasn't a talker, there was something about his calm attitude that left Lovina yearning for more time with him.

One evening, Lovina baked a plate of her famous homemade ginger snap cookies and decided to take a few across the creek as a thank you for Luke's help in the garden.

Knocking on the shed door, she cautiously pushed it open, cheerfully announcing, "Hello! Luke! Are ya in here?"

"*Jah*, I'm here," Luke replied.

There he was, standing next to a work bench with a busted buggy wheel laid out in front of him.

"Hi there!" Lovina greeted him, suddenly feeling unsure of herself and terribly bashful, "I thought I might bring you something." Placing the plate of cookies on the work table, she watched Luke eyeball them before picking one up and putting it in his mouth.

"It's just a thank you for all the help you've been giving me," she explained.

Luke raised his eyebrows and nodded as he swallowed, "*Danki* – they're very good. You're a good baker, Lovina."

Lovina felt her heart skip a beat with his compliment. Looking at the work he was doing, she added, "Looks like you've got quite a few talents of your own."

Reaching for another cookie, Luke gave a shrug, "I keep busy for sure....but that's a good thing. I'm always thankful for the money."

Leaning back against the table, Lovina studied him in the growing darkness, "Saving back for a farm of your own?"

Luke stared straight at his work and shook his head, "No. I'm going to give my money to help out my family. I have no need of a place of my own."

"Don't you ever hope to get married and have a family?"

Luke shook his head slowly, "I'm afraid all of my dreams are gone. I plan to be alone forever."

His words broke Lovina's heart. Although he tried to sound resolved, it was easy to hear the pain in his voice.

"*Ach*, Luke," she managed to whisper with a smile, "Don't say that. You never know what might happen."

Luke took in a deep breath and then let it out slowly. Looking up to meet Lovina's eyes, he studied her for what seemed minutes before asking, "What about you? Do you think that you could ever love someone like me?"

His question took Lovina by such surprise that she almost fell over. Her eyes growing large, she looked down at the floor, her heart flooded by a million different emotions.

"I...I...Luke..." Lovina's voice was trailing in every direction but her words were making no sense at all.

"Lovina," Reaching out, Luke put his hand on top of hers, "Would you consider going with me to the singing after church this weekend?"

It felt like Lovina would not be able to breath, so many decisions were running helter-skelter through her mind. Almost a surprise to herself, she heard her voice say, "Sure. I don't see why not."

Although David had been staying busy with the horses, he still managed to make some time to help out in the store. With a beautiful girl like Hannah there, he had to find time to spend with her.

One afternoon they had received a large order of supplies and were hurrying to put them on the shelves before it would be too dark to see, even by the glow of the lantern.

"*Ach*, this is a job!" David grumbled as he hurried to put some bags of flour in their place on a shelf, "Of course this would just happen to be the night that Uncle Amos and his entire family went visiting...leaving you and me to do all the work."

Hannah smiled and shook her head, "David, you complain so much. I don't mind the work. Work keeps me busy...work keeps my mind off of...other things."

Suddenly interested, David looked up in surprise. Maybe he would finally have a chance to hear some of the secrets that were hidden away behind this mysterious girl's sad blue eyes.

"What other things?" David asked.

Hannah shrugged as she ran her fingers over a bag of sugar, "Disappointments...heartbreaks...bad decisions."

Hannah went silent, assuring David that he would hear no more of her story, but then she surprised him when she went on to clear her throat and say, "I had a boyfriend...a fiancé even."

As the words came pouring out of her mouth, it was easy to see that they were tearing her apart. Hannah closed her eyes and continued, "But things didn't work out. We were engaged but...well, I was filled with so many uncertainties. I called off the wedding before it was even announced in church. I didn't mean to end everything with him – I just needed more time to think. But I'm afraid he took it as an outright rejection. And now, I'll never have a chance with him again," Hannah reached up to wipe away the tears that were threatening to overwhelm her, "*Ach*, David, it almost breaks my heart to talk about it. I have destroyed all my chances for happiness."

Looking at her in the light of the lantern, her face clouded over with pain and tears gathering in her eyes, David felt totally broken for her. Pulling himself to his feet, he stood up straight and stepped closer to her, putting a hand on her thin shoulder.

"Hannah," he whispered her name with all the tenderness that he had been storing in his heart, "Dear Hannah...you still have a thousand chances for happiness." Reaching up, he took his thumb and brushed a tear off of her cheek.

Hannah took a deep breath and let it out slowly. Looking at him in surprise, she simply whispered, "*Danki*, David." Then she squared her shoulders and announced, "Let's get back to work."

Chapter Six

Over the next few days, David and Hannah had little time to spend together. He looked forward to ever chance he had to see her. Although their friendship had not had time to progress, David felt confident that over the rest of the summer he could easily earn himself a special place in Hannah's lonely heart.

One afternoon, David had finally found a chance to work in the dry goods store alongside Hannah when one of his cousins came rushing into the shed with a letter in his outstretched hand.

"David," the little cousin called out, "You got some mail!"

Taking the letter, David quickly recognized the handwriting as that of his younger sister, Lydia.

Ripping the seal open, David pulled out the letter, unsure why his teenage sister would even take the time to write him.

Dear David,

I don't want to bother you while you're gone, but I need to let you know something important. I've always thought that you and Lovina had something special together, although I'm not sure if you had any kind of plans for the future or an agreement. While you've been gone, Lovina has taken a spark to the very man you sent here to work – Luke Christner. Seems like they're seeing each other almost every day and last night I overheard him invite her to the singing Sunday night. She agreed to go with him.

I don't mean to stick my nose in where it doesn't belong, but I know that you were always sweet on Lovina and just thought you should know.

Your sister,

Lydia

"*Ach,*" David read over the letter and then reread it again, his heart suddenly dropping into his stomach.

Lovina – with Luke? A multitude of emotions suddenly assailed David. He found himself so frustrated, almost angry at Luke for stealing his girl. How dare Luke go to David's own home and try to take the woman he loved away from him? David was hurt, so hurt, by Lovina's decision to move forward with a relationship with someone else. But, worst of all, David felt incredible guilt and sadness.

Deep in his heart, David realized that it was his own fault that Lovina and Luke were growing close. In all the time that David had been in Indiana, he had never taken the time to even write his childhood sweetheart a letter – he had just always taken for granted that she would be there for him when he returned.

While he had been busy pursing a friendship with Hannah, he had never thought that Lovina might be looking at someone else.

Reaching up, David rubbed his hand across his face, trying to gather his wits and decide what to do next.

"What is wrong, David?" Hannah asked softly as she stepped up next to him.

David balled his free hand up into a fist, fighting the urge to destroy the letter he had just received. Passing it to Hannah, he quickly explained, "I don't know how to tell you this, Hannah, but Lovina...well, she and I have always been friends. I don't mean to have led you astray in any way because I have liked you since the day we met but this..." David couldn't go on.

Hannah took the letter in her own hands and read it slowly, her eyes growing large as she went over the message again and again.

"David," she managed to breath softly, "What are you going to do?"

David brushed his hand through his hair as memories of Lovina ran across his mind, "I don't know. I just don't know." Turning, he gave the floor a hard kick with the toe of his boot.

"David," Hannah took a deep breath and shook her head slowly, "I hate to say this, but you know that we aren't meant to be together. No matter how happy we might have both been to pretend...it just isn't so. You have made my summer much more enjoyable...but it's time to get back to our real lives."

David looked down at his feet. He wanted to fight her words; he hated the idea of giving Hannah up completely. But, when he thought of his dear Lovina...he knew that he couldn't live without her.

"Go to her, David!" Hannah exclaimed, "Go to Lovina and let her know that you love her."

Taking a deep breath, David nodded his head, "I'll go call a driver right now."

Chapter Seven

David sat in the passenger seat of the truck, half-heartedly listening as his driver talked incessantly during the long trip back home. Looking out the window, David watched the scenery slowly change from the flat Amish country of Indiana to the rolling hills of Kentucky.

With each mile that passed, it seemed that David got even more nervous about his future with Lovina.

When he first started home, he had been certain that she would be glad to see him but now...well, the closer he got to her, the less sure he became. Maybe she had truly fallen for Luke and she wouldn't want to even see him. Maybe David had blown his one and only chance for true love with the only girl he ever truly cared for.

Lovina had just filled up a bucket of water and got down on her knees to scrub the kitchen floor with a scrub brush when she heard a truck pull up in the front yard.

Ach, Lovina thought to herself as she plunged her hands down into the soapy water, *Daed must have visitors.*

It was Saturday afternoon and Lovina found her mind plagued with thoughts of Luke and their upcoming date. Although she truly enjoyed spending time with him, there was something about agreeing to go on a date with him that put her mind entirely in a tizzy. As much as she liked Luke and was attracted to him, Lovina battled thoughts of David – it seemed so sad to be turning her back on their relationship with each other.

But, she reasoned to herself, when she thought back on it, she and David had never had a true relationship. Sure, he had always been a good friend to her, but it seemed that was all things were to ever be. Since he left for Indiana, she had not heard a word from him and, as sad as she was to admit it, she was starting to wonder if he would ever come home at all.

"Lovina."

The voice seemed to come out of no where. Lovina looked up in surprise, wondering if she was truly hearing a person or if it was her own imagination.

There, standing in the doorway to the kitchen, was David himself.

"David!" Lovina managed to breathe as she struggled to pull herself to her feet, "Oh, David...is that really you?"

In an instant, David had bridged the space between them. He came right to her side, nearly knocking her bucket of soapy water over in his hurry.

"Lovina," David managed to say, somewhat louder this time, "Lovina..." he seemed to want to say more, but acted as if he couldn't find the words. Reaching out, he grabbed Lovina and gathered her into his arms.

To Lovina, everything felt like a crazy dream. Pressed firmly against her old friend's body, all thoughts of Luke vanished from her mind as she let David hold her like a little girl.

"Lovina," David pulled back only long enough to kiss her on the mouth, "Lovina, I have been a total moron. I am so sorry!"

"David," Lovina managed to say as she tried to catch her breath, "David...what has happened?"

David stepped back as he struggled to gather his composure. Reaching up, he wiped away at tears that threatened to overtake him.

"Lovina," he reached out and held her hands in his own, "I have been so ignorant. I left home, anxious to find adventure and experience new things...and I almost lost the one thing that means the most to me in the world – you."

Lovina felt her heart start to melt as David poured out his soul to her, "Lovina, I love you. I love you more than I ever realized. I thought that Uncle Amos was giving me a chance to experience adventure but I think it was actually the good Lord allowing me the opportunity to realize how much I love you. Please, Lovina...I don't want to wait any longer. Say that you will marry me!"

There had never been anything that Lovina wanted more. In that instant, it felt like all of her hopes and dreams were finally coming true.

Luke.

The name entered her mind suddenly and it felt like the life was drained right out of her. Oh, but hadn't she already led him to believe that she cared for him? Hadn't she already agreed to go out on a date with him this very weekend?

"David," Lovina squeezed her dear friend's hands tightly as she looked for the right words to share her news, "David. I have been a foolish girl."

"And I have been a foolish man," David was quick to add.

Lovina smiled and shook her head, "Perhaps we've both been foolish..."

Her words were cut short as the sound of an approaching vehicle brought them both from their thoughts.

Glancing out the window, they watched together as a strange car stopped in front of the house and let out a passenger.

David felt his heart sink when he saw the visitor who was getting out of the strange car.

It was Hannah.

David thought that she had understood. What was she doing...following him all the way to Kentucky of all places? Hadn't she been the one who had said that their relationship wasn't going to work and even pushed him to return to Lovina? What was she doing here now?

David battled the urge to run forward and stop her before she could get to the house. Turning to Lovina, he struggled to find the words to explain what was surely about to come.

"Lovina..." he hurried to say, "While I was gone, I was an idiot. I hate telling you this more than you will ever know, but I got involved with a girl from Indiana. We never started to court, but we were heading in that direction when I heard that you and Luke had begun a relationship...."

As the words poured from his mouth, David watched Lovina's face turn ashen and then red with shame.

"You already know about Luke?" She managed to whisper.

David nodded his head, "That was the wake-up call I needed. That was what I needed to bring me back home. I never want to risk losing you again, Lovina!"

Lovina started to wipe tears away from her eyes, "David, I don't want to lose you either! But what you heard is true. Luke and I have grown close and are on the verge of starting a relationship. I was so foolish, David, but I was afraid I had lost you and now I don't know what to do..."

In the other room, they could hear a knock on the front door.

Wiping at her eyes, Lovina hurried to go open it with David trailing close behind. When she opened the door, Hannah was standing on the front porch, a determined look in her blue eyes.

"I need to talk to David," she announced, looking from Lovina to David.

"David," she took a deep breath, "I need to go to your house...I need to see Luke."

Luke? David was more confused than ever. Cocking his head to one side, he tried to understand where this strange twist came into play.

"You don't have to look far," the deep voice of Luke spoke out and they all turned in surprise to find that he had come up on the porch and was standing just out of view.

"Hannah," as he said the name, his voice seemed to fill with a strange sort of pain.

"*Ach*, Luke..." Hannah looked down at her black shoes as if she couldn't hold his gaze, "I have been wanting to talk to you."

Luke shook his head sadly, "I can't imagine what we would have to say to each other now."

"Luke...you know that I am a very shy girl," Hannah said in a shaky voice, "And I have let my fear get the better of me far too many times. I almost let it destroy what we had together. But Luke...I can't let that happen."

David's eyes got large as he realized that Luke must be the ex-beau that Hannah had told him about.

"I love you, Luke," Hannah announced resolutely, "I love you and I still want to be your wife...if you can ever find it in your heart to have me."

David watched Luke and held his breath, hoping that he would agree.

Stepping forward, Luke reached out and took Hannah in his arms, "I love you too, Hannah!" He exclaimed as he cupped her face in his hands, "I have always loved you and I always will." Turning to look at Lovina, he quickly tried to explain, "Lovina, I hope that you understand..."

Lovina smiled broadly as she wrapped her arms around David's waist, "It is fine, Luke. I think that things are exactly the way that they are supposed to be!"

Epilogue

Standing together at the kitchen sink, Lovina and David watched as a group of children played outside in their front yard.

"Look at those crazy things," Lovina muttered as she noticed her daughter trying to climb a tree.

"Just like us when we were little," David announced.

Lovina looked up at him and smirked, "*Jah* – and I think our little girl might have a crush on the neighbor boy, as well."

David and Lovina had now been married for ten years and had three children of their own. It had been a double wedding shared with Hannah and Luke, who decided to move to Kentucky so that Luke would continue to enjoy a steady stream of work.

David and Lovina had built their house behind his parents' place and, to their surprise, Hannah and Luke had bought a piece of farm land right across the creek.

Their children played together and it wouldn't be any surprise if someday those same children would grow up to marry one another.

David smiled broadly and gathered his wife up in his arms.

"I'm glad I went to Indiana that summer," he announced as he reached out to push a strand of her brown hair back from her face, "Because that summer showed me how much I need you in my life."

Bending over, he gave her a gentle kiss.

Life truly was as David and Lovina had always imagined it – and they were happier than they ever could have guessed possible.

THE END

IN THE AMISH WIND

MEGHAN MASON

The wind was blowing fiercely, making the clapboard shutters on the old farmhouse bang against the windows. Leah sat up in bed stock straight, always jumping at the slightest sound during the night hours. It had been three long, torturous months since her daughter, Lara, had up and run off to marry some Englischer. It was on a night such as this very night, with the wind howling, and the rainstorms threatening to open over the fields, that Lara had chosen her path. As soon as young Lara, only sixteen years old, had laid eyes on that outsider, trouble had been afoot in the Johnson household in the small, quiet Amish community in the otherwise peaceful countryside of Pennsylvania. Lara had apparently wanted a new life, separate from the Amish traditions and faith that her parents had worked so diligently to instill in their offspring. It was every Amish family's worst nightmare to have one of their own abandon what values they held so precious. But for Lara's mother, this loss had been especially harsh, as Leah had prayed for a daughter since she had been a young girl, always dreaming of passing on the religious faith, as well as the respectably simple yet hard working lifestyle of the Amish. Lara had obviously dreamt of something far different, leaving Leah to sob at the loss of her only daughter.

With the wind becoming more threatening, Leah woke her husband, Simon, from a sound sleep, and asked that he go check the shutters to make sure the old farmhouse was indeed ready for the approaching storm. Simon did as his wife requested, as he always did, wanting to reassure her of their family's safety. Simon also felt the loss of Lara, but not as acutely as her mamm. Simon had the two sons to help with farm chores and mold into proper Amish young men. Jonas and Jeremiah were dependable, reliable, and loyal sons, and Simon intended to focus all his energy into raising fine young farmers to carry on the family livelihood. As Simon pulled up his suspenders, he grabbed hold of his hat, and walked hurriedly towards the front door. He did not notice that Marmalade, the family's big fluffy orange tabby, also making his way towards the front door. As Simon yanked at the door, despite the overwhelming power of the wind, out ran Marmalade! Simon spied him too late, as he followed the cat out into the fields. The weather conditions and dark of night did not help Simon in his quest to bring Marmalade back to shelter. Simon had taken a lantern, but it had blown from his grip almost immediately upon stepping outside. Poor Marmalade was not going to fare very well out in this weather, and he shuddered at what Leah would say once she found out that her beloved cat had now absconded much the same way his daughter had three months past. With that grim thought, Simon checked the security of the window shutters, and went back inside the house. By this time, Leah had gotten up, and was busily preparing a hot pot of tea for Simon,

"Simon, was everything secured from the outside? I don't want to be caught unawares when the downpour starts. This old house has so many creaking boards and spooky noises that my nerves are on edge." Simon knew that Leah had been much more prone to worry since they had lost Lara. He dreaded having to announce that Marmalade was now the latest family member to abscond in the dark of a stormy night. This was going to upset Leah to no end, but it was better to simply get it over with, than to wait for his poor wife to go calling for her cat in the morning, only to discover he had run off,

"Leah, I am afraid I have some bad news about Marmalade. He ran outside when I opened the door, and I could not find him anywhere."

"Oh no! Not my Marmalade! Please, Simon, not my Marmalade! He is my comfort nowadays, since Lara left us. He curls right up to me, and always senses my moods. How could he just run off like that in this terrible weather? Doesn't he have a lick of sense?" answered a distraught Leah.

"He's just a cat, Leah. Let it be," tried Simon, but the instant the words left his mouth, he knew he had said the wrong thing. His wife had loved the old cat with her whole heart. Some people were just born to understand animals, and Leah had certainly been one of them. After Lara had gone away, Leah would talk to Marmalade while doing the household choring, or take him out to the garden with her to keep her company. Simon could understand how this relationship with a cat was better than solitude. Without the menfolk around during the day, Marmalade was all she really had. Simon felt awful that he had not been able to capture Marmalade,

"I'll go out now, and try to look for him, Leah," he offered. So, Simon stood up from his tea, and off he went into the cold, stormy night to hunt down a scared and probably very wet housecat.

Leah moped around the kitchen for the two and a half hours that Simon was out searching. Then she began to think about Lara, and how much she missed her daughter. How could Gott allow this to happen? This was the constant question that ran through her head. She had lived a righteous enough life, had followed in her own mother's footsteps and had become a dutiful Amish wife. She had born her husband children, and worked hard to make a happy home for everyone in the family. So why did Lara forsake them all for the life of the Englisch? Leah was no better off than she had been the morning after Lara's disappearance. Three months was arguably not very long, and one could hardly blame her for mourning the loss of her daughter, but it was beginning to destroy Leah. She was tired all the time, she was plagued by unsettling dreams, if she could sleep at all, and she had even stopped attending services on a regular basis. She found herself making up an excuse of illness, or a headache, or simple exhaustion to remain at home. Simon and the boys would attend church services alone, and people would ask after her with concern, knowing that her only daughter had run off. During this time, she would take to her bed with Marmalade curled up at her feet. She would cry into her pillow, begging Gott to hear her prayers, and send Lara back home. But, the days had grown into months, and still no Lara. It felt as though Gott was not listening, or if he was, then maybe he did not care. Almost as if breaking the spell of sadness that was now a regular part of Leah's daily life, the creak of the front door jarred her back to reality.

Simon reported no success at finding any trace of Marmalade. He had called and called, listening for his meow, but nothing could really be heard beyond the roar of the wind and the cracks of thunder. Simon was now drenched from the rain, and stood by his wife, trying to provide some semblance of comfort. He knew how despondent his wife would be, now that the cat was gone too. He was at a loss as to how to help her, and knew that this would be yet another painful loss for Leah. In an attempt at comfort, he poured a shallow dish of melke and set it out under the eave, where there was some protection from the weather. Maybe katze like faithful Marmalade would double back in search for sustenance. He figured that was their only hope. With that taken care of, Simon and Leah checked on the boys, and returned to bed. There was little else to be done, but sit tight and see if the cat would make his way back home.

It was still gray and drizzling the next morning, but the wind had died down considerably, as Leah stood at the kitchen sink washing up the breakfast dishes. She stared out the window that overlooked the garden, hoping and praying that Marmalade would show up. But, she had been up for hours, and still no sign of her orange cat. Simon had long been gone, and taken Jonas and Jeremiah with him to survey the damage of the fields. He said he'd keep an eye open for Marmalade, but she knew he had much more important things on his mind. Her missing cat was bound to be her worry, and her worry alone. After all, Simon had given up on Lara, and an errant cat was not going to fare much better than a runaway daughter. As she washed and dried the dishes, Leah indulged herself in a lovely daydream of looking out that front window only to see Lara sitting there on the bench, her chestnut colored hair tied neatly in a bun, her Amish blue dress pressed nicely, and her white apron filled with the green beans she had just picked from the garden that mother and daughter had planted together. And there next to her darling Lara, sat a purring Marmalade, batting bugs with his paws, and chasing his tail. But Leah knew this was just another silly daydream. She had heard through various people from the Englisch town that Lara and that man of hers were doing well, and seemed to be happy enough. There was very little chance that her mother would ever see Lara again. Once an Amish girl left the fold, the Amish community was not very keen on welcoming visitors that had turned their back on their way of life. Despite her pain at losing her only daughter, Leah knew better than anyone that she must come to grips with the fact that Lara was gone for good. She just did not know or understand how she was supposed to do this. She was ashamed that she still blamed Gott for Lara's own choice. Gott gave his people free will, and Lara had certainly exercised hers. Still, there were times when Leah just began to cry, looking up to the Heavens, and asked Gott why he had allowed this to happen, even though she knew the ridiculous nature of the accusation. Gott was there to hear the prayers of the faithful, not to withstand the blame of the actions of his flock. Lara had been the only one to blame, and the sooner Leah came to grips with that fact the better off she would be.

At half past one, after the men had come in from the fields for lunch, Leah decided to go wandering around the village to look for her cat. She could hardly stand there and accept that Marmalade was gone, when he might be scared and alone somewhere. She owed him at least a few hours of her day to search. He had to be around somewhere. Perhaps he took shelter in a barn on someone else's property during that awful storm, or maybe someone had taken him in, thinking that he was an unfortunate stray. Leah hoped that the latter was true, rather than entertain the thought that some terrible fate had befallen her beloved cat. She pushed those negative and destructive thoughts out of her head, adjusted her bonnet, and went in search of her loyal friend. Leah made a silent and secret promise to herself that she would not stop looking for Marmalade until she had proof that he was no longer alive. How could she abandon hope for her furry companion, when he had always been by her side? Leah's daed had picked him special for her out of Bruder Franklin's busslin. His mouser had just had a mess of babies, and her daed had brought home that small ball of orange fur just for her. It was a rare show of affection from her daed, and she had treasured the gift as much as the gesture. Her mamm had thought the gift foolish for a young girl who had chores and responsibilities. Leah had come from a very large family of eleven siblings, so her mamm's opinion was that she hardly needed one more thing to take care of, Leah being second to oldest. But, Leah had raised that tiny kitten in addition to all her daily choring, and had taken the cat with her when she married Simon.

Thankfully, today was a bit brighter than the preceding stormy days, so at least it would be a bit easier to look for Marmalade. There were no howls of the wind to compete with, or torrential downpour. Leah began her search just around the nearest parts of the house, hoping against hope that her cat was still nearby. Perhaps he was hiding in the bushes near the garden, or over by the barn. She called to him over and over with no reply. So, the next step was to expand her perimeter, and head north towards the neighbors' farms, as to the south there was nothing more than crops. Leah trudged over hills and into valleys, as she made the rather arduous hike across the entire village. She asked any passerby whether they had spied an orange tabby cat, but still she had no luck. She was feeling so discouraged. With no cat in tow, she gave up the hunt, as she had to get home to ready the supper. Simon and the boys would soon be returning from their day in the fields. Hungry menfolk would not understand if she were not there, and no food was on the table.

By the time she reached her own little house, it was beginning to get dark, and the storm clouds were slowly rolling in. Now she had the added stress of wondering what to prepare with so little time at her disposal. She decided the best course of action was to make a hodge podge of some sort, with boiled vegetables and the leftover meat from last night's dinner. There were already freshly baked rolls from this morning, when she had had some extra time after cleaning. It would not be her best meal presentation, but it would have to suffice. She had spent all afternoon outdoors, neglecting her regular day to day duties. She would have to hurry along to arrive home first, and be able to make it appear as though she had not been out very long. Leah sprinted across the back of the property, and slipped through the back door. She got to work immediately preparing the stew, and praying it would not be served up too late. She purposefully chose a variety of softer vegetables that would take less time to boil. After what felt like mere seconds, Simon, Jonas, and Jeremiah arrived, talking animatedly about something they had found by the door. Her heart leapt, as she hoped it was her cat. To her surprise and curiosity, Simon produced an envelope,

"This letter was attached to the front door, Leah. It appears that it was hand delivered sometime today. Did anyone come calling or knock at the door?"

"No, it's just been me alone," answered his wife. Simon opened the letter, and found that it was from Lara! Inside, the letter was addressed to Leah, so he gladly handed the note to his wife. He was disgruntled that Lara and her escape were still making waves of stress and discomfort within the family, and retreated to the back of the house to clean himself up for the evening meal.

The note was rather short, and Leah tried to read her daughter's scrawling handwriting while tears poured from her eyes. She was trying to finish making the stew at the same time, but the gist of the note stated that she was doing fine, and that a boppli was on the way! It was to be expected early fall, and she wrote that Leah was welcome to visit her in her new home in town. Leah had so many mixed feelings at this news, but duty called, and dinner must be set. She cleared the table, set it, and called her husband and sons to supper. After the grace was said, Leah could not contain herself,

"Simon, Lara has written that she and her Englischman are expecting a dear little boppli! This is a perfect example of how a girl needs her mamm! Instead, she will spend her pregnancy away from her relatives, and I will likely miss the birth," she cried out.

"Enough of this! I will not have my home life disturbed by a daughter that felt her life would be better outside of the Amish ways! Leah, you will stop this worrying immediately. These three months have changed you, and you need to move on, or none of us will ever be able to lead a normal life!" Simon was angry now, and Leah knew his limits, but she could not hold back ant longer,

"Simon! How can you be so cold towards your own flesh and blood? We are to be grandparents, and I for one, am not about to ignore that fact!" Leah responded with a raised voice. She knew that Simon had been pushed to his limit, and sensed what was about to be said,

"I told you to leave the situation alone," Simon was now almost yelling, and the boys looked extremely uncomfortable, "Die Zeit fer in Bett is nau!" Simon rarely used the traditional old German of the Amish, and Leah knew that he meant business. He had ordered her to retire to the bedroom and go straight to bed. She knew that Simon had lost his temper. She got up, leaving her dinner things at her place, and ran to her room. If Simon wanted to act this way, then so be it. He and the boys would not enjoy having to clean up the supper things, but he had given his angry orders that she was to get ready for bed early. She sobbed as she changed to her night dress, and folded the letter up into a tiny square. She carefully hid it in one of her dresser drawers so that she would not lose track of the address that Lara had given. It was her only hope of ever seeing her grandbaby someday! Leah tossed and turned, at times praying her hardest to Gott that everything would somehow work itself out for the best. She begged Gott to keep Lara safe during her pregnancy, and then turned her worried thoughts to Marmalade! She prayed yet again, that Gott would see fit to lead her cat back home.

She knew that her faith was wavering, and that was not a good thing at a time such as this. Leah knew from years of experience and church lectures, that one must allow Gott to lead the way. Her faith was the cornerstone of her Amish way of life, and she knew she must remain strong if she was to get through all of these troubles. Simon's order to go to bed early proved a blessing, as this gave her private time with her thoughts and time for prayer.

By the time morning came, she awoke late, noting that Simon was already gone out to the fields. She went to check on her sons, and found that they too had gone out with their daed. Simon had allowed her the luxury of sleep, and had obviously gotten his own breakfast in order to let her rest. Lord knew she needed it, but at the same time, she felt pangs of guilt creeping in at not being able to focus her energies on running her home properly. Leah set to choring right away, because she understood that enough was enough. She had no desire to upset her husband further, and felt strongly that her boys deserved better maternal affection than she had given them as of late. She cleaned the kitchen from top to bottom, did the laundry, and prepared the lunch. After all that, Leah took out her sewing basket to do some mending. This gave her some time to sit still and think over the events of the past, and try to come to peace of mind. Things could not afford to continue in this vain, as her family needed her to be a strong part of the household, a proper wife, and a loving mother. As she continued with her sewing, Leah resolved to turn over a new leaf, and remain strong in her religious convictions that Gott would lead the way in whatever way He saw fit. She knew she had to learn to let go of control, and allow her faith to lead the way. Lara was old enough to bear her own bopplis, and she had already proven herself able to fend for herself in the outside world. As her mother, Leah would have to allow Lara the benefit of the doubt, and let that part of her sorrow dissipate. After all, there was to be a boppli born, and she knew she could take outings to the village to visit with Lara now that she knew her address. At least there was that hope. As for Marmalade, she would continue the hunt this weekend, once there were less chores to complete. She could not neglect her responsibilities no matter how much she missed her animal friend. She must have faith that Marmalade was out exploring the big wide world, and that he would find his way home if he desired. After all, he had a pretty good life here at the farm with Leah fulfilling his every need.

The weekend finally came, and Leah bundled up to go cat hunting. She even packed a bit of kitty kibble to jiggle along the way in hopes of drawing him out of hiding. The best path was likely up the hill towards the next farmhouse. This belonged to the Jamison family, and they were the local dairy farmers. They served the Amish population's needs for milk, butter, cheese, and other dairy products, and she happened to know the farmer's wife from their church services. Maybe Mary Jamison had seen Marmalade sneaking around the barn searching for melke. As Leah rounded the bend that lead to the Jamison property, she spied a small child of about five playing in the distance. Once she got a little closer, she noticed the child was a little girl, and that she was happily playing a game of catch the mouse with none other than a big orange tabby! At last Marmalade had been found, and best of all, he was happy and playing with his new little friend. Leah's heart simultaneously jumped for joy and felt a pang of jealousy. Why had Marmalade abandoned the farm in search for another owner? This thought was of course ridiculous, as Leah reeled her emotions in, as she knew that pets were known to make an escape for whatever strange reason. They did not think or reason the way humans had the capacity, so she had to calm down, and visit Mary before she took any action. She turned away from the little one and the cat, and resumed her way up the path to the house. It was much larger than her own, given that the Jamison's provided dairy for the entire community. Leah also knew that Mary had about six children of varying ages, and that one son resided at home with his growing family. It must be a bustling and busy household, she thought to herself, as she knocked upon the door.

Mary answered the door, and promptly invited her Amish schwester inside for the customary cup of tea and offer of food. Leah made herself at home at the kitchen table as Mary prepared the tea and cake,

"Mary, I come visiting today because I have lost my cat Marmalade. He's been missing since the storm last weekend, and I've been out searching for what feels like forever. I am grateful to have spotted him playing out in the yard with a little girl. Is she your own?"

"Why yes, that would be little Rachael, my grandbaby. She is my son's daughter, and lives here with us while their barn is being built. Does that big orange cat belong to you, Leah?"

"Yes, I am sure it is my Marmalade, but now there is the problem of taking away Rachael's new friend. I am not sure that would be for the best. It is true enough that Marmalade has been a wonderful part of our family, but maybe this is a sign that it is time for Marmalade to move on to another owner who maybe needs his love even more than I do," replied Leah. After all, the little girl had looked so happy playing with the cat. How on earth could she remove him from the child, and potentially break her heart? Certainly, no good would come of that tactic. She could see that her cat was being well cared for, and was not being neglected or mistreated in any way. In fact, she had not seen him this active and playful in many years! Perhaps she should discuss the matter further with Mary,

"Rachael appears to be a very sweet little girl. You must be so happy to have her so near. I just heard from Lara, and as you know, she left us some three months back. I just received word that I too am going to be a grand mamm! I hadn't expected that news at all, so that was a big surprise!"

Mary knew that Lara had gone off, and felt very sorry for Leah,

"Oh, that is good news, although I am sure it has upset Simon, no doubt."

"Well, yes, of course you know how stubborn he can be at times, but I pray he comes around to the idea. I plan to visit Lara in town once the boppli arrives. Perhaps, if the visit goes well, I can make regular trips to see her and the boppli. That is something too important to miss," suggested Leah. It was then that she led into the subject of Marmalade,

"Mary, do you think it best to leave Marmalade with Rachael, if you are willing to allow the child to have a pet? I cannot break the heart of a child."

"I would allow Rachael to keep the cat, but would not want that to upset you. I can only imagine how you have been worrying over him since the storm," offered Mary, as she slid her friend another slice of cake,

"That decision would be up to you, Leah. You've had your share of troubles lately, and we don't want to be the cause of any further upset. I do know that there is a newly born batch of busslin two farms over, and that we could always return your cat to you, and go choose another for Rachael." At that very moment, in came a giggling Rachael awkwardly carrying the big furry cat,

"Hello, Miss Leah! Look at my new friend, Mr. Pickles! He came last week, and I made him a bed in my room. Want to come see it? I sewed the bedding myself, and every night I tuck him in." Leah could not resist humoring Rachael, so off they all went down the hall to the little girl's room to see Mr. Pickles' new bed. It was adorable the way that Racheal had set up her doll bed to serve as the new bed for the cat. She looked at Marmalade, who was now apparently known as Mr. Pickles, and saw that he was enjoying being so pampered,

"It's time for Mr. Pickles to take his morning nap while I help grand mamm make the lunch!" she explained, as she carefully tucked the large orange ball of fur into his bed of fluffy covers. Mr. Pickles had obviously tired himself out playing in the yard, and was now making himself comfortable in his doll bed. It was one of the cutest things Leah had ever seen!

"We had better leave Mr. Pickles to have his nap, so he won't be a grumpy kitty later," announced Leah. There was now no question that she must relinquish her at to Rachael for this new chapter in his life, and in her own. If there were baby busslin to choose from, then Leah would march over to that farm and claim one for herself. She could see that Rachael was a sweet care taker, and felt happy that Marmalade had found a new home, and that he was indeed safe. That had been her biggest fear. That poor Marmalade had befallen some awful fate during the storm, but somehow, he had found his way here, and was now enjoying the attentions of the little girl,

"Mary, I must be going now, as I think I must stop off at Bruder Feldman's," said Leah, giving Mary a knowing look, as Mary gave Leah a smile. As she left the Jamison house, she felt confident that her cat was being well cared for and given lots of love. She made her way further down the road to the Feldman's to see if she could pick out a brand-new kitten.

Leah arrived at Bruder Feldman's farm twenty minutes later, with her heart bursting at the seams with a mixture of happiness and loss. She was sad to lose her Marmalade, but overjoyed that he was now with a sweet and loving little girl. Marmalade had needed to move on for whatever reason, and now it was her turn to do the same. She greeted Bruder Feldman, and she inquired after the busslin. He happily guided her towards the barn loft, where Missy, his mouser, had given birth just weeks before,

"Leah, my dear schwester, just go on up to the loft, and choose any kitten you want. There are six of them little critters to choose from. It'll be hard to pick just one," he chuckled merrily. As she reached the top rung of the ladder that led to the loft, she spied the busslin nursing from Missy. They were all a mix of brown and white, except for one tiny one on the very end. That kitten was pure white with a little spot of very light orange on her chest. Leah knew that was the kitten she must have. The white signified the purity of new beginnings, and the spot of orange was a small reminder of her old life. She instantly scooped her up, and spoke to the tiny animal,

"I will call you Hope, because that is what I thought I had lost when Lara left, and then Marmalade. You are the smallest kitten who looks like you need the most care, so I will choose you." Then she carefully and lovingly wrapped Hope within the fold of her apron, and climbed down the loft ladder. She thanked Bruder Feldman, and began her journey home. She held Hope close, so there was no chance she would fall out and get injured.

A few hours later, Leah had returned home with a little bundle wrapped inside her apron. Simon, Jonas and Jeremiah were all seated at the kitchen table, probably asking themselves where she had gone off to this late in the afternoon. They had already seen the baked goods she had prepared early that morning, and smelled the simmering soup that was prepping for supper,

"Leah! Where have you been? We were beginning to worry," began Simon, but Leah cut him off,

"Oh Simon! I am sorry that I have been such a difficult mess lately. I went looking for Marmalade, but Gott has answered so many of my prayers by sending me instead to Bruder Feldman's." She unwrapped her apron, and out popped the little head of Hope. Jonas and Jeremiah gathered round to admire the cute little addition to their family, and Simon looked at his wife with wide-eyed wonder at how all this had come about,

"Simon, I have resolved to begin life anew, and I have come to terms with Lara's departure. She will still have the help and love of her mother once the boppli is born. I have decided that every other week, I will make the trip into Englisch town to visit with her and the grandbaby. You may come or stay as you wish, but I am determined to accept all of this for the betterment of our family. Little Hope, here, was also an answer to my prayers. I sought to bring home Marmalade and resume my old life, but found him to be in the care of a very special little child. Mary Jamison told me that Bruder Feldman had a group of busslin, so off I went! This is the special kitten that I chose, and named her Hope. That is the best name I could think of when I laid eyes on her!" exclaimed Leah. She saw that her husband gave a small smile, as he was not one to show excessive emotion. She knew that it was his seal of approval, and she felt that Simon would eventually agree to accompany her to see Lara someday.

The spring and summer months passed, and Leah and Simon received word from town that Lara had given birth to a healthy boppli girl. She had named the boppli after her mother, and this made Leah weep tears of happiness. Her daughter loved her after all, and she could hardly wait to travel to town to see her daughter and the new little Leah. At this happy news, Leah started work sewing the boppli's new gown, and gathering a basket filled with homemade jams and treats. She also hunted through her old trunk, and discovered an old dolly that had belonged to her daughter. She spruced it up the best she could, made the doll a fresh dress and bonnet, and added the gift to the top of the basket.

Simon had already been up early the next weekend, hitching the buggy to the horses for their family trip into town. The whole family was going, and Jonas and Jeremiah had gathered wildflowers for their sister, and had crafted a nice sturdy tool box for the Englischer that no one had yet met. They hoped that he would accept the offering as a sign of acceptance. As the buggy carried them along the dusty roads, Leah looked out upon the green and gold fields of crops, and admired the hard work of her Amish bruders and schwesters. Even though they had a daughter who was not a part of their faith any longer, Lara was still going to be an important part of their lives. She gazed up at the clear blue sky, and gave a silent prayer of thanksgiving to Gott, who had somehow led her here to this special day. She heard a small meow, and glanced back at Jonas who was minding Hope, as she rode along with the family in her own special basket. Leah was thankful and filled with gratitude for her new beginning, and for the unconditional love of her family. But, most of all, her faltering faith had been restored through constant prayer and trust that Gott had a special plan for her life. She no longer felt insignificant or sad or lonely. All she felt was Hope.

HANNAH'S AMISH BABY

PHYLLIS ROGERS

The scent of white oak filled the tiny wood shed Samuel Fisher worked in. It was a pleasant herbal-like aroma with nutty overtones. He hand-cut each piece of wood and smoothed them with a wood planer his father and grandfather used before him. He used a lathe to form the spindles, which he fit into the sides of the cradle, one by one.

Samuel took off his black straw hat and wiped the sweat off of his head and face. It had been a grueling two months. It seemed as though the drought had settled and was there to stay. The farm work had become arduous, and between the long days of working in the fields with the blistering heat and taking care of his beloved wife, Hannah, the young man sometimes was overwhelmed. He paused and sighed, concerned. Hannah's pregnancy had proved to be a difficult one. It was the hottest summer on record. The lack of air conditioning offered little respite for one in such a state. Hannah had lost their first child at only two months. She was much further along this time, and the doctor monitored Hannah and the baby carefully. He told her constantly to take it easy. Thankfully, Hannah's mother, Sarah, was able to help. She and Hannah's father, Jacob, were nearby in the main house, while Samuel and Hannah lived in the smaller cottage which had been built a few feet from the back door.

Samuel returned his attention to the wood. He had cut a white oak tree at the far side of the farm, which spanned seventy-five acres. The graying white bark had V-shaped patches and ridges. The characteristics of the wood blended well with the simple furniture he and his forebears had constructed.

Samuel intended the cradle as a surprise to Hannah. He devoted an hour each afternoon to working on the project and wanted it to be perfect.

There were times he questioned his competency as a husband and father. He had lost his own parents when he was young, and he wasn't really taught what it was to be a man. Hannah's father was the best example he had in that light. He deeply respected Hannah's father as did all the local Amish folk, however, Samuel often felt as though he lived in Jacob's shadow. Jacob seemed to do everything right. He was a loving pillar in their community and often thought of as a leader of sorts. Samuel wasn't sure if he could ever be the man Jacob was.

The cradle was an offering of love and devotion to his wife and unborn child. Samuel sanded the wood down to a smooth, soft finish and laid it carefully on his work table until the next day's work.

"*Liebchen*," Samuel whispered to Hannah as he went into their tiny cottage and kissed her on the forehead.

She was working on a quilt for the baby. The quilt had larger squares which had alternating white hearts at the centers, and every other square had smaller pastel squares sewn into an "X" shape. The colors used were yellow, blue, pink, and green. Whether Hannah had a baby girl or a baby boy, the quilt would be perfect. She placed the quilt she was piecing together on the table in front of her and turned her attention to Samuel.

"*Mann*. How did today go?" Hannah inquired.

"The heat is slowing us down," Samuel admitted. "All we can do is pray for rain and for fall to come quickly."

"Yah," Hannah agreed.

Samuel washed up and helped Hannah to her feet as they made their way to the main house for dinner.

"*Maemm*," the two said to Sarah as they found their way to the dining room table. Jacob joined his family and led them in prayer as they held hands in a circle around the table. They sat and prayed in silence until Jacob said, "Amen."

Sarah prepared a delicious meal, as always. They passed around the shepherd's pie and sauerkraut, while a peach pie awaited them for dessert. Though Sarah loved taking care of her family and preparing meals, it had become a more grueling task recently, given the lack of good, cool air.

The men didn't think about the heat during dinnertime. The long days of hard work kept their appetites going, and Hannah was always hungry these days. She was eating for two now.

***

Jacob arose at 4 a.m. as he often did and sat in his rocking chair as he read his Bible. He searched for answers to assure himself that things would improve, and that the drought would end soon. As head of the house, he felt responsible for his loved ones, but ultimately he knew it was all in God's hands. Still, everyone looked to him to be the calm and rational one in times of trouble. He sought comfort and strength through God in his daily Bible readings. As he finished reading the book of Jeremiah, he joined Sarah in the kitchen as she prepared breakfast.

"*Gute Mariye*," she greeted him with a smile.

Sarah felt total joy in each day. She arose each morning and saw them as new beginnings full of promise and hope.

"*Gute Mariye*," Jacob echoed as he hugged her gently, pressing his hollowed cheekbones over hers. His demeanor was always strong, yet gentle.

"Dr. Stotzfus will be coming today to check on our Hannah," Sarah informed Jacob.

"*Gut*."

Jacob grabbed his hat from the peg near the front door, and rushed out after eating the breakfast Sarah had prepared for him. There was much to be done, and he wanted to make as much progress as possible before the stifling heat set in and slowed them down. He headed towards the barn to milk the cows. Samuel did most of the heavier work on the farm, while Jacob did lighter chores these days. Some days they worked together out in the fields.

It was only six in the morning, but the excess milk had to be delivered to the dumping station by 9 a.m. They kept only enough milk for the day and sold or gave away the rest. The few dollars they earned from the milk and eggs he collected were enough to keep them going, especially since the drought made the harvest so meager.

"That's a girl," he told the first cow as he pulled on its udders. They didn't have modern equipment to milk the cows as some of the locals did. Samuel hadn't given into the temptation to modernize. He gently patted the first cow before going on to the next. He steadfastly ignored the twinge he felt in his chest as he got up.

"It's just a little indigestion," he assured himself. He had eaten too much scrapple for breakfast, he thought as the pain passed. He had more work to do. The animals needed to be fed, and their pens needed to be cleaned.

Though some of the animals had to be sold from time to time, and some had been lost to the heat, there were a good many animals to care for on the farm. There were cows, goats, sheep, and chickens. The chickens laid fewer and fewer eggs during the oppressive heat, which almost didn't justify the cost on feed for them. Jacob remained optimistic and looked for better days. He had run the farm for a long time. He knew the drought would pass and better seasons would come.

***

Hannah arose and prepared for her visit with Dr. Stotzfus. She pulled her long auburn locks back away from her freckled face and fastened her hair into a bun at the back of her head. She then placed her white prayer cap over her head. She was anxious to see what the doctor had to say on his visit with her.

Dr. Stotzfus was a balding man of short stature, but a jovial fellow. He was raised Amish but had left the church to join the military and received his medical training there. When his career in the Army was over, he returned to serve the community as a doctor. He was one of the few in the area who had the modern conveniences of an automobile and a phone. He drove around to all of the homes in the community that needed his services. He faithfully kept watch over Hannah to help prevent another miscarriage.

He carefully examined Hannah and listened to both her and the baby's heartbeats. He took some of her blood with a syringe and did a couple of tests with some small machines he brought to the visit. His jolly demeanor turned to one of concern.

"I'm worried about your sugar levels and the amount of fluid your body is holding, Hannah."

He tried not to sound too alarmed, but Sarah could tell that he was.

"I'm going to check on you three times a week from now on, but in the meantime, I need for you to follow this diet," he said as he handed her a list. "And stay off your feet! You need to elevate your legs and rest."

He pulled Sarah aside and told him that Hannah had pre-gestational diabetes as well as signs of pre-eclampsia. Sarah was familiar with pre-eclampsia as she herself had lost a child due to having the condition. He told her that if Hannah were to get much worse, she'd probably need to be monitored closer to a hospital, so it was of utmost importance that she was taken care of appropriately. He knew Sarah did all of the cooking for Hannah, so he gave her special instructions - lots of meat, vegetables, minimum starches and sugar, and foods that had a lot of iron as Hannah was also anemic. He handed her a bottle of iron pills.

"*Denki*, doctor," Sarah said as she ushered Dr. Stotzfus to the door and handed him a couple of loaves of bread and some eggs. "Don't worry. I will take care of our Hannah."

Sarah returned to Hannah's side. Hannah grew weary of all the rest time, but she took the doctor's concerns to heart. She didn't want lose this baby too.

"Trust in God and lean not into thy own understanding," Sarah told her. "It will all be okay."

***

Samuel was back in his tiny woodshed working on the cradle. He had meticulously carved a hummingbird into the headboard. He knew Hannah loved hummingbirds, and it was a nice, added touch. He screwed the side panels of the cradle to the headboard and footboard. The bottom panel was secured by joints. He sanded the finish one more time and applied a coat of oil. He decided the color was perfect as it was. The cradle was finished. He looked at the cradle from side to side and top to bottom.

"*Gut,*" he said to himself, satisfied with his work. His next project would be to build a frame swing that he could put the cradle on. He mopped the sweat from his brow.

"Another day," he said. "Another day."

Samuel whistled as he made his way out of the wood shed towards the house. He was happy with his surprise for Hannah. There weren't as many flowers along the path because of the lack of rain, but there was a huge mound of bright yellow Black Eyed Susan flowers. They had black centers and the flower heads were each about four inches across. Hannah had sowed the seeds herself along with many of the other garden flowers on the property. The Black Eyed Susan blooms didn't seem to mind the dry dust as much as the other flowers that had diminished.

Samuel paused to pick a few of the large yellow flowers for Hannah. He loved to make her happy, and there was so little to do that these days. The heat was hard on everyone, but especially hard on Hannah as the idleness proved difficult on her.

"*Liebchen,*" he greeted Hannah as he pecked her dimpled cheek and handed her the flowers.

Hannah's face lit up.

"*Denki.*"

Sarah decided to bring dinner to Hannah and Samuel, in an effort to minimize Hannah's walking. She prepared an iron-rich meal to help with Hannah's anemia – liver pudding, sauerkraut, and shoofly pie. The molasses pie had a lot of iron and would comfort and soothe Hannah's weary body. Hannah was not fond of liver pudding, however, and turned her nose up at the sight of it. She felt bad for doing so as Sarah worked so hard to help them, and Hannah quickly corrected herself.

"*Denki, Maemm*," Hannah said trying to sound more grateful as she restored her smile.

"I'll get the dishes in the morning," Sarah said on her way out of the cottage.

"You've been coming in a little later these days," Hannah quizzed Samuel.

"*Yah*," Samuel admitted. "There are a couple of smaller projects on the farm that I've been working on, but I'm almost done. You'll soon have more time to grow tired of me again," he said with a smile as he picked up their dinner plates.

"Never," Hannah said. "I don't know if that could ever happen."

Samuel brought the dishes to the kitchen, and Hannah started to join him. He motioned her back to elevate her legs as the doctor ordered, much to her disappointment.

"I'm so tired of just laying around," she exclaimed.

Hannah was accustomed to hard work. She was bored and restless.

"You won't be laying around for long, *liebchen*. You'll soon have plenty to do," Samuel promised as he kissed her forehead.

Samuel took the checkerboard from the table in the living area and brought it to Hannah so they could play a game. He was intent on distracting her from her boredom.

"I win again," she said.

"Ah, so you do."

"Perhaps you are letting me win so many games? Could that be, *Mann*?"

"Nope. You won fair and square."

There had been times Samuel purposefully put little effort out to score a victory, but this was not one of them. He normally gave

Hannah a run for her money, but he was tired and ready for bed. He extinguished the oil lamp and lay down next to Hannah.

"*Guten Nacht*," Samuel said affectionately as he kissed Hannah on the forehead.

"*Guten Nacht*."

***

Jacob lit the kerosene lamp as he made his way to his rocking chair. Though he had a full night's sleep, he was quite tired and felt somewhat under the weather. He held the Bible he had read from since he was a little boy and faithfully read from its pages. He had drawn strength from the Bible many times in his life, and he had learned the evening before from Sarah of the challenges faced by Hannah and her pregnancy. He had faith that God would see her through this. Everything seemed overwhelming at times – the drought and heat, the farm, Hannah's difficulties – but he knew it would all work out in the end, in God's timing.

It was a day that Samuel and Jacob were to work together in the fields. The fencing needed repair, as some of the animals had made their way out of the property. Sarah packed them a peanut butter sandwich lunch so they wouldn't have to make the long walk in the heat until they were finished for the day.

"*Gott* be with you," Sarah faithfully told him as she walked him to the door. She sighed as she lost sight of him, knowing the day would not be easy for him. They were not spring chickens anymore, and the heat did not help things. She pulled the crisp white curtains back to usher in the morning sun and went to check on Hannah.

The two men met each other in the pasture. Samuel had filled the wagon with fence posts, slats of wood, nails, hammers and other supplies. He pulled the wagon as they made their way through the farmland. The sun was rising and the widening crystal blue sky offered a panoramic view. The once fertile pasture was becoming more barren, and the cornstalks which grew the feed for the animals were more spindly and parched, but the farm was still a beautiful, peaceful place.

Jacob had worked the land all of his life. It was his gold and in his blood. He couldn't deny it was getting harder and harder. He was thankful to have the help of his son-in-law. He wouldn't have made those past few months without Samuel.

They pounded fence posts into the ground and drove nails where it was needed. There was a lot of fencing to cover. They worked relentlessly to get it all done.

As the day wore on, an orange haze cast itself over the farm and the fields. It was blistering hot in the afternoons. The men took a break under a large tree, which shaded them some from the heat.

"I'm really proud of the work you are doing on the farm," Jacob said to Samuel.

The compliment caught Samuel off guard. He looked up to Jacob and it meant a lot to him that Jacob noticed his efforts.

"*Denki*, sir," Samuel nodded.

"One day, this will be yours and Hannah's. You've earned it for sure."

Samuel had lost his parents to an accident when he was younger. They were in their buggy on the road when a truck hit them head-on. Samuel was the youngest, and his older siblings raised him with the help of an aunt and uncle who lived nearby. It was a logical choice to live with Hannah's parents on their farm when the invitation was extended as everyone else seemed to have a place, and Hannah's parents needed help on the farm.

The men drank from their thermos bottles and tried to save some water for the walk home. It would seem like a longer stretch since it was later and hotter, and they were more tired. As they made their way back, Jacob's breathing grew labored. He tried to convince himself that it was normal given the circumstances, and he pressed on. He paused a moment and rested his hands above his knees as he tried to catch his breath. His chest felt heavy, and he couldn't speak. He waved at Samuel as he grabbed his chest. Helplessly, Samuel watched Jacob crumble to the ground.

There was nothing Samuel could do. He was in shock. Hannah's father was gone. He felt the weight of the world on his shoulders. He didn't want to have to tell Hannah. This would crush her.

Samuel carried Jacob back home on the empty wagon from which he had dumped the remaining supplies. He tried to wipe the tears which flowed from his face. He needed to be strong for the women.

Sarah looked through the window and saw Samuel pulling the wagon with Jacob stretched across it. She let out a gasp and ran to them. Samuel explained what had happened in a low voice. Sarah allowed herself a moment of grief, but turned her attention to Hannah. How could she tell her in such a fragile state?

"We must be strong for Hannah," Sarah gently ordered Samuel.

He nodded in agreement, wiping away his tears.

***

Funerals were about the only time the small Amish communities stepped away from the tradition of wearing their simple, light colored clothing. The women wore black, and those closest to the family wore it for an extended period of time.

Hundreds of people from around the local Amish communities went to the farm for Jacob's funeral. Hannah's and Samuel's siblings had come out early to set up seating and food areas, from the barn to the house. Jacob's body was placed in a simple pine coffin, which rested in the middle of the living room of his and Sarah's home. People payed their respects and told many stories of Jacob, filled with their fond memories of him, then made their way out where guests visited and ate. A simple spread of cold cuts, cheeses, breads, vegetables, and pies lined the tables. Everyone pitched in and took the burden off of Sarah and

Hannah. Hannah was allowed a break from bed rest for the day, but Samuel and Sarah monitored her closely to be sure she didn't overdo it.

When the time came to bury Jacob, a procession formed for the ride out to the nearby cemetery. Samuel helped Hannah and Sarah into their buggy as they led dozens of horses and buggies toward the burial ground. He suppressed his emotions, but Jacob's passing had rattled Samuel, bringing back strong memories of losing his own parents.

The cemetery was a beautiful spot and a weak breeze occasionally blew through the grounds, lending a scant respite from the heat. All of the headstones were plain, unmarked, white stones in keeping with the Amish tradition.

The minister spoke a little, and the ritual concluded with the funeral goers chanting the words to the hymn, "Nearer, My God, to thee":

"Or if, on joyful wing, cleaving the sky,
Sun, moon, and stars forgot, upward I fly,
Still all my song shall be,
Nearer, my God, to thee;
Nearer, my God, to thee, nearer to thee!"

***

Two weeks had passed since Jacob's burial. Sarah spoke to Samuel and Hannah during dinner concerning a decision she made.

"It is time for me to live in the cottage and for the two of you to move into the main home. It is as it should be, and your father would want the same thing. It's time for a new generation to make their home here."

It was also Sarah's way of trying to make Samuel feel more comfortable as the new head of the household. The young couple conceded to Sarah's request. There was not much to move as they lived a simple life and did not have many personal belongings. Samuel moved what little there was while Sarah visited with Hannah.

"*Maemm*, are you sure this is what you want?"

"Of course, my Hannah. This is as it should be. And I will be right at your back door should you need me," she offered with a smile as they held each other's hand.

Sarah was a pillar of strength and faith. She fully believed that everything happened had a reason, and she trusted in God's plan for all things.

After Samuel moved things from one house to the other, there was one last thing to bring into the main house. He felt it was the right time to surprise Hannah with the cradle he made for their baby.

"For you, my *liebchen*, and our baby."

Hannah's eyes filled with tears. The cradle was more beautiful than she would have hoped for. She realized this was probably what Samuel was doing all those evenings he returned home later than expected.

"It's beautiful. I love it. *Denki*."

Samuel placed the cradle in their new bedroom off to the side and noticed a chest that was left behind. As he started to carry it out to Sarah's new home, she stopped him.

"It is mostly heirlooms. Some were Hannah's when she was younger, including some clothes that will be perfect for the baby. Leave it here."

Samuel nodded and left the chest in its place. Everything was moved from one house to the other, and Sarah kissed them as she made her way back to her tiny new home, but not before reminding Hannah to rest.

"Remember to take it easy, my Hannah."

"I will, *Maemm*."

"And I will be sure she does," Samuel promised.

***

Time was getting closer to the baby's arrival. Dr. Stotzfus remained alarmed over a few things concerning Hannah and the baby, but things had not progressed as badly as he had feared. He was more hopeful than he had been that Hannah could safely deliver her child.

Samuel had neighboring helpers on certain days to help with the farm chores, but he handled much of the farm responsibilities on his own. It was Sarah's job to continue looking after Hannah until the baby arrived.

It was August, and there were not too many more hot days left for the Pennsylvania summer. Rain had fallen too infrequently and the crops continued to struggle. Samuel wondered if he should bother planting the winter crops. He was not as confident in his decision making as Jacob always seemed to be. Some of the wheels for the buggy needed to be replaced, the barn was in need of repair, a new well needed to be dug, and more. The canned goods in the cellar were depleted as there was less to preserve. There was so much that needed to be done and not very much money, time, or manpower. Expecting a baby added more to the urgency of it all. He felt responsible for his family and wanted to make the best decisions.

Samuel stopped the plow and grabbed his suspender as he looked out into the fields. Composing himself, he prayed silently:

"Make me the man you intend for me to be. Make me a man that Hannah can be proud of. Help me to be half the man Jacob was. Please look after Hannah and help all to go well with her and the baby. Amen."

He unleashed his burdens to God and felt somewhat better, as he continued plowing the fields. He made his way home, and he saw that Hannah going through the heirloom chest that her mother left behind for them.

"Hannah," he said. "Should you be out of bed?"

"It's only for a little while," she assured him. "I get so tired of doing nothing all day."

Samuel noticed the doll that Hannah was holding. It was a muslin doll with a blue dress and a white pinafore fashioned over the long sleeved underdress. The doll had a black bonnet and no eyes or lips.

Hannah had received the doll one Christmas, and it was tucked away once she outgrew it.

She had once asked her father why the doll had no face? Jacob told her it was because everyone looked the same to God, and he loved everyone equally. Jacob had asked Sarah to sew a wooden button at the center of the pinafore, after he had carved an "H" at the center, which stood for "Hannah."

"I had almost forgotten about this doll all these years," Hannah told Samuel as tears flooded her face. Finding the doll had unleashed a wash of memories of her father's kindness and wisdom.

"Do you ever wish our faith allowed us to have photographs, Samuel?"

The question surprised Samuel.

"If we had photographs, it would be something we could remember our loved ones by," she reasoned. "Then I could see my father every day and you could see your parents."

"Perhaps," he told her. "But we can keep our memories of them in our hearts," he told Hannah as he lay his hand over her chest.

"*Yah*," she agreed as she placed the doll back in the chest.

***

Hannah woke just before daybreak with labor pains. It was not supposed to happen yet. The expected delivery date was still two to three weeks out.

"*Bobbel*," she yelled and awoke Samuel. "Baby is coming!"

Samuel leapt from the bed and assured Hannah that everything would be ok. He lit the kerosene lamp and told Hannah he was running to the cottage to get Sarah. Deep down, Samuel was frightened. He knew it was too early and with the difficulties she had experienced during the pregnancy, he knew Hannah would be too. He collected himself quickly, because he knew he had to be strong for the women and most especially, Hannah.

Sarah rushed to Hannah's side. Her water had not broken yet, and Hannah's contractions were still far enough apart to get help, Sarah hoped. Sarah had assisted in home births before, but she didn't want to take a chance with Hannah.

"Go, as fast as you can and get Dr. Stotzfus," she quietly told Samuel. "But first, put a pot of water boiling on the woodstove."

Dr. Stotzfus lived three miles away and whether Samuel ran or took the buggy, it would take him about a half hour to reach Dr. Stotzfus. At least with a car, it would only take Dr. Stotzfus five minutes to return.

Sarah's attention focused on Hannah. Hannah held her breath out of instinct, but Sarah told her to breathe.

"Slow, deep breaths, my Hannah," she gently ordered.

"I didn't know it could hurt so much, *Maemm*," Hannah said.

"Of course, it hurts, my Hannah. But when it's all over with, you will quickly forget the pain," Sarah promised.

Hannah was supine on the bed. Sarah had learned through many births this position was okay until the birth pains got closer. Then, Hannah would have to sit up.

The contractions soon grew closer, three minutes apart. Sarah figured Hannah was mostly dilated, but her water still had not broken. This worried Sarah. She knew the water should have broken by now. She hoped Samuel would soon arrive with Dr. Stotzfus.

Hannah's breathing quickened, and she panted furiously, while sweat poured from her face. Sarah grabbed a towel and dipped it in cool water, as she gently dabbed the damp towel over Hannah's face.

"You are doing well. You are doing well, my brave Hannah. Just try to slow your breathing down a little bit," Sarah requested.

At that moment, Hannah's water broke, and the labor pains were very close together. The baby began to crown, and Sarah knew it would not be long before the baby would be born.

"Slow, deep breath, then one big push," Sarah told Hannah.

Hannah pushed hard and let out a scream as the baby made its entrance into the world. Samuel and Dr. Dr. Stotzfus entered

the room just as it happened. They rushed to Hannah's side, and after a quick check, Dr. Stotzfus assured everyone that both Hannah and baby were okay.

"Looks like you two ladies didn't need me after all," Dr. Stotzfus chuckled.

"Hannah and Samuel – you have a little baby girl," Dr. Stotzfus announced as he wiped the baby clean and cut the umbilical cord. Sarah wrapped the baby in a blanket and handed her to Hannah.

"Now you will know what it's like to love someone more than anything else in the world," she told Hannah.

Samuel and Sarah sat on either side of Hannah, proudly smiling from ear to ear at the events of the morning. The sun was rising, the birds were trilling their songs, and a new life had come into the world.

"What shall we name her?" Samuel asked.

"How about Ruth?" Sarah nudged. "After your mother, Samuel."

Samuel had no words. He was twelve when he lost his mother, and he couldn't think of a more perfect way to honor her.

"Ruth, it is." Samuel and Hannah were both touched by Sarah's thoughtfulness.

Samuel went to the heirloom chest and retrieved the doll that was Hannah's when she was a little girl. Since they had a little girl, it was fitting for it to be handed down to baby Ruth. Hannah agreed and the doll would stay with baby Ruth in her cradle until she was old enough to play with it.

***

Baby Ruth was growing and healthy. Days were more normal at the Fisher farm. Hannah was able to help her mother with chores to help keep the homestead going, and Samuel was busy working the farm and planting crops. The days were getting cooler, but rain was still scarce and threatening production of the crops.

Hannah became more concerned that Samuel wasn't being decisive enough about the problems that plagued the farm. She worried more about things now that she was a mother.

"*Maemm*," she told her mom. "We have very few canned goods left, and I think Samuel could use help on the farm, but he insists on doing it all."

They always had a bounty of jars filling the cellar. They had canned most of their vegetables, and fruits from their trees, as well as some of the meat from their animals. They didn't have a freezer as some of the neighbors did. So they relied on the food they produced and preserved to survive, but the months of the drought affected their stock.

"Not to worry, Hannah," her mother told her. "God always provides."

"But *Daat* wouldn't have let things get to this place," Hannah responded.

Sarah raised her eyebrows in surprise. "Patience! It will all happen in good time. Your father had years of experience. Samuel is just learning to be his own man, and he didn't have always have a father to teach him. Give him time and trust your husband and God."

"I will try," Hannah agreed.

The women continued their Saturday work. It was the day of the week when they dusted all of the furniture and mopped all of the wood floors. It was a tradition they did together, both helping the other with their houses.

Later in the evening, Sarah told the young couple that they should devote time to each other alone, and she would watch baby Ruth. It had been a while since the young couple had spent some time together, and Sarah hoped the evening together would be good for them. She didn't mind the extra time with her granddaughter either.

Samuel had a surprise for Hannah. He had waited for a moment such as this. He lured her into the pasture, where he had nailed sheets between two trees. He parked the buggy out in front of the sheets, and there was a projector that he rigged to a car battery. He had found the items in a junk heap in the barn. He played Charlie Chaplin's film, "The Kid", over the projector and handed Hannah a paper bag filled with popcorn.

Hannah had only been to the picture show one time during Rumspringa when she was a teenager. During that time in her adolescence, she was permitted to spend the weekend at a cousin's house, whose family was part of a more liberal Mennonite community. There, she had watched "The Wizard of Oz." She had been amused, then, at the idea that Dorothy would laugh at the two men below in the boat as she was hurled into the tornado. She couldn't deny the movie was entertaining.

"Samuel, should we…" She was unsure of doing this. She was always taught to follow the Amish customs, and many didn't agree with the idea of watching films.

"I think it's okay. Don't worry," he told her.

Apprehension gave way to laughter as they watched the silent film star and his slapstick antics come alive on the makeshift screen.

The young parents settled into one another's arms as they watched the movie and ate popcorn. It was the most fun they had in a long time.

The next morning, Hannah went to get baby Ruth from Sarah, and Hannah reluctantly told her mom what happened the night before.

"I know *Daed* would be so disappointed, and we shouldn't have done that, *Maemm*, but…"

Sarah laughed and interrupted Hannah before she could finish.

"Where do you think all that stuff came from, dear? Your father did the same thing with me when we were about your age."

Then they both chuckled and made no mention of it again.

***

The holidays were coming up and Samuel continued to feel pressure about the lack of goods and funds for the homestead. He confided in Sarah about his worries. It was not a common thing for an Amish head of household to do, but Samuel felt comfortable speaking to Sarah about it.

"Jacob and I had the same trials and hardships when we were younger," Sarah shared with him.

"How did you get through it?" Samuel listened intently.

"Well, at times Jacob handled things without me knowing what he had done, but I do know that he sold trees off the property. It would tidy us over nicely."

Samuel had not thought of that. Suddenly, he felt a bit of hope for their situation.

He sold a few walnut trees at the far side of the property and received a generous sum. The wood made from the trees was in high demand and yielded a pretty good return. The loss of the trees hardly put a dent in the forested part of their land, and they were left with enough money to make necessary repairs around the farm, as well as fill their cellar until there were better times for the crops. Samuel also purchased a few things that made chores easier around the house and farm.

There was a good bit of money left, and Samuel wanted to bring the family to town to get things they needed. Hannah had gotten into quilting in a big way and decided she wanted to sell her creations, so she needed more supplies. Sarah gave them her blessing, and decided to stay home for the evening.

Samuel parked their horse and buggy along the path of the street as the family strolled the town. Baby Ruth was in a strolling carriage, and Hannah and Samuel pushed her as they enjoyed the sights of the town. It was nice to get away.

Hannah found her way into a shop that offered some beautiful fabric that she would enjoy fashioning some of their wardrobe items with as well as items that were perfect for quilting. She picked a few things out for Sarah as well.

Samuel enjoyed spoiling her that evening. They ended the day at a nice restaurant, which they had not done before as a new family. As they left the restaurant, they saw a flash of light from the corner of their eyes. It was a traveling photographer taking a photograph of a young family.

The flash of light jolted a memory from Hannah's mind. She remembered a time when as a young girl, about five or six, she and her father had come into town just as she had with her little family. She was drawn to the same kind of flash of light and asked her father about it. He had allowed them to be photographed, and she remembered him placing the picture in a pocket that was on the dress of the muslin doll that had been Hannah's.

She remembered it all so vividly, yet wasn't sure if her memory was playing tricks on her. She picked up the muslin doll from Ruth's stroller where it rested, looking for a pocket.

There it was – a photo of Hannah and her dad. The photograph she once wished she had of her father when he passed away was near her all the while and now in her hands.

Hannah and Samuel smiled as they looked at the picture and read each other's minds. They had their photograph taken, along with baby Ruth, so that she would one day have a memento of their little family. Though they did not go so far as to display it, they could not believe that such a beautiful moment captured in time was truly part of the forbidden tree they had heard of their whole life.

HANNAH

<u>December</u>

The service had been lovely as always but Hannah had been unable to concentrate, her mind bustling with dozens of thoughts. As she followed her fiancé's family from the home of one of the member and into the back area of their farm, she wrung her hands nervously.

"Hannah, are you unwell?" She jumped at the sound of Isaac's voice near her ear.

"Not at all! On the contrary, in fact," she replied, peering at him, confusion coloring her face. "What would make you ask such a thing?"

"You seemed not to be paying any attention whatsoever during the sermon. I believe the Bishop scowled at you at one moment." Shocked, Hannah paused in mid step to stare at her husband-to-be, abruptly holding up the line trekking through the field.

"You must be joking!" she cried and then saw the twinkle in Isaac's gentle hazel eyes.

"Perhaps I am but you must admit that your mind has been elsewhere today. What are you thinking about? I noticed the faraway look in your eye from my side of the room!" Hannah laughed and continued toward the barn where the Fisher family had arranged for lunch following their Sunday worship. The winter had been unseasonably warm and Hannah felt somewhat overdressed in her wool cloak. She wished for snow. It did not feel festive without snowflakes gracing the air.

"Well? What is it that plagues your thoughts? Are you reconsidering our marriage?" Again, Isaac's warm eyes lit up with laughter and Hannah grinned broadly at his jesting.

"Certainly not! I am simply concerned about Christmas," Hannah replied, her thoughts beginning to race once more. It was Isaac's turn to show confusion.

"What of Christmas? It is the loveliest time of year. Surely you can't be glum!"

"Not in the least," Hannah replied as they made their way into the spacious structure to join the rest of the congregation. "I am simply worried I have not prepared properly. I have made presents of all of the children and for my parents but I feel as though I have forgotten someone. Which brings me to the Christmas cards. I am always concerned that I have left out a family. Can you imagine how much embarrassment that would bring to us should I omit a single family? What's more is I set up the nativity scene in the front of our home and I cannot find one wise man and two angels. Now I suspect that Rachel has been playing with them but I have yet to find them and she denies knowing their whereabouts. I must have father whittle some for me or else it will be a disaster!"

Suddenly Hannah felt as though a huge weight had been lifted off her shoulders with the confession. Isaac burst into laughter.

"Oh, Hannah! The things which make you fret do amuse me endlessly. It is Christmastime, *liebchen*. It is not a time of worry and fret. That is for the English. We are only to give thanks and spend time with those dearest to us."

"I know, Isaac, but I cannot help wanting Christmas to be perfect! It is my favorite time of the year. And look! This year we haven't even any snow! It hardly seems proper to even set up a tree without the candlelight twinkling off the snow." Hannah pouted but immediately smiled as the truth of his words struck her. Of course he was right; this was not a time of stress. Their way was that of peace and order, not to be overshadowed by the trivialities which the outside word concerned themselves. It was what made the Amish community so special; the ability to block out the unnecessary and focus on the beauty of the basics in life. Hannah could not be happier. She and Isaac had become betrothed in February and their impending marriage was announced to the community in October as per tradition. They had plans to wed the following winter as per tradition and she could not have hoped for a better mate. Despite their engagement, Isaac continued to act as though they were newly enamored with one another, bequeathing her with beautiful flowers and penning poetry for her, words which made her warm to her soul. She was excited to begin her life with him. It seemed that the wedding was millennia away, not merely a year.

"Ah, Hannah, you may worry but your Christmas spirit is infectious," Bishop Philips told her, overhearing the last of their conversation. Blushing scarlet, Hannah turned to acknowledge him, bowing her head.

"Your sermon was well received today, Bishop," Hannah told him, trying to recover from her embarrassment. "It is a rare treat to hear you speak lately. I'm afraid we miss hearing your voice in service. I am pleasantly surprised you have joined us today."

"Unfortunately, I have had business in other districts as of late but I am happy to be back at home. I haven't had the opportunity to congratulate on your betrothal. Isaac, you have done well for yourself. The Yoder family is well respected in our district. Perhaps you will bless them with a son." The Bishop smiled at the couple.

"Not that the Yoder women are any less hard working than any of the men in our community. How is your family? I do not see your father here today," the Bishop continued, looking about, a sudden cloud covering his brown eyes. Hannah and Isaac followed his gaze. Hannah's mother, Ruth stood speaking with several other women while her sisters, Rachel and Miriam ran through the barn, playing a game of tag with some of the other children. As the three continued to look about, Hannah felt a stab of panic in her stomach. It was unheard of for her father, Mark to be absent from church services. She had spent the previous week in Isaac's district at a family member's home. Hannah had been slowly learning the workings of his father's farm at the insistence of Mark who thought it best she understood the complexities of her husband's land as much as possible. As Hannah's cousins resided in close proximity to Isaac's farm, the transition had been seamless and it allowed for their sweet courtship to continue uninterrupted. This also meant, however, that Hannah was not as informed as to the comings and goings of her own family. Brow furrowed, Hannah excused herself and hurried over to her mother, despite Isaac's reactionary hand on her arm to stop her.

"*Mamm*, where is *Daed*?" she whispered in her mother's ear urgently without preamble. Ruth gave Hannah a reproving look and politely exited the conversation in which she was involved.

"Mind your manners, Hannah!" Ruth Yoder chided her daughter.

"I'm sorry Mammi, I am just worried about him. It is unlike him to miss service. I can't recall one instance prior to this one in fact!" Hannah insisted. Seeing her oldest daughter's distress, Ruth's face softened.

"Your father was away at market in Pittsburgh over the weekend. He was expecting to be back last night but the weather turned so he must have been detained. He will likely be home when we return." Hannah exhaled with relief and returned to her fiancé and the Bishop where she reiterated what she had been told. A bell rang to indicate that the meal was about to be served and they all sat at the long tables set up in the middle of building. Yet as they bowed their heads and grace was said, once again, Hannah felt herself distracted by unstoppable thoughts. This time, however, they were not of snowfalls and wise men. Suddenly she her mind was focussed completely on the whereabouts of her father.

"I don't mind, Hannah but I cannot help but feel you are overreacting somewhat," Isaac informed her as they pulled their carriage toward the Yoder farm.

"He is my father. I must know that he is well, Isaac," Hannah replied.

"*Liebchen*, he has been going to market since well before you were born. I am sure he is well. You will see." Isaac smiled boyishly at her and encouraged the horses onward. Hannah felt an uncharacteristic smidgen of annoyance at his placation. She gave him a sidelong look but said nothing. She hoped he was right but some inherent sense told her something was amiss. Inclement weather or not, Mark Yoder would have been at worship. His devotion to God was his priority, probably above his own health and safety. Hannah knew her father. He would have risked riding in a blizzard to honor his commitment to the community. Her mother had arrived back from the Miller farm with Rachel and Miriam and the pale afternoon light was already becoming dark, forsaking dusk altogether.

"I do not see his wagon," Hannah mumbled as they pulled to a stop. Alarm growing in her chest, Hannah recognized the Bishop's carriage which was parked behind the modest house. Hannah did not wait for Isaac to escort her from her seat and instead was running up the front steps to toward the door. As she flew inside the house, she stopped in her tracks. Her mother was on her knees, surrounded by Rachel and Miriam, a look of shock upon their faces. Tears had slipped from their cheeks to the wood floor. Bishop Phillips stood, solemn faced at the base of the stairs, his hat in his hands, his lips pursed into a fine line. They did not need to speak. Hannah already knew.

January

"Hannah, Isaac came calling again," Miriam told her, pushing open the door to the bedroom where her sister sat brushing her long hair, placing it into sections for braiding. Hannah did not respond. Instead she continued to count the strokes, slowly, meticulously smoothing down the strands.

"Hannah? Hannah!" Miriam strode into the room and snatched the utensil from her sister's grip. The older girl looked up in surprise and instinctively grabbed it back.

"What is it?" she demanded, rising to her feet menacingly.

"Isaac was here," Miriam said again. "He would like you to contact him when you are well."

"I am well, thank you. I am simply busy. With *Daed* in the hospital, fighting for his life, someone needs to help *Mamm* run the farm, Miriam. I cannot up and run off to help him when Isaac has able bodied brothers there. What does he want from me?" Her words were like a torrent of venom and twelve-year-old Miriam stepped back, shocked at her tone.

"I believe that he wants to know if you're well, Hannah. I don't think he wants you to help him on the farm," she offered, timidly, tears filling her eyes. Hannah was immediately contrite but her anger would not lessen.

"Thank you, Miriam. I will be in contact with Isaac shortly." Her sister immediately retreated from the bedroom, closing the door in her wake but Hannah heard her sister's stifled sob before she retreated down the stairs. Hannah knew that her tone had been unreasonably harsh but she could not seem to alleviate the insurmountable rage which had filled her since the horrendous accident her father had endured a mere month before. The driver who had injured Mark so severely on that lone road heading home from the city had yet to be caught and Hannah knew she would not rest until the person had been apprehended and brought to justice. Christmas had come and gone in an unmemorable blur, still filled with family and friends but in a much more somber tone than the joy of the season typically brought. The family had left the candles lit in the windows well after other members of the community had extinguished theirs, a constant flame for others to keep Mark in their prayers. Hannah remembered thinking that the nativity scene was ruined and she had reprimanded Rachel harshly for playing with the wooden characters, reducing the child to a blubbering mess. Much more than that, Hannah could not recall about holiday. There had been an exchange of gifts but Mark's had lay unopened at the hearth and Hannah did not have any recollection of what she had received. Hannah's mother had continued her duty, tending to the farm and caring for the children and Hannah had stepped in to assist as opposed to joining Isaac. At first, Isaac had attempted to stay nearby, offering his unselfish aide to the Yoder family but eventually Hannah's increasingly sullen behavior had driven him home to his family's land. Still, he had frequently visited his beloved to see how she was faring. More often than not, Hannah made herself unavailable for reasons no one could comprehend. While she never admitted it to anyone, she blamed Isaac also for her father's fate. *If only he had been more vigilante, heeded my words more carefully when I suggested that something was amiss with father,* she told herself time and again. It did not matter that Mark Yoder had been hit on the Saturday night, well before Hannah had any inkling that there was trouble. In Hannah's grief she was beyond reason and all she had remaining was her intense anger. It was irrelevant whom was the recipient of her rage. It needed to be released and Hannah ensured that it was so. Mark's initial prognosis had been grim. The internal damage to his organs was severe and he had several broken bones. He was still on a life support machine in the hospital where he had been taken following being struck. Hannah could not bear to see her strong, vital father in such a condition and had refused to attend his side despite her mother's pleading.

"Hannah, your father needs you there," Ruth had begged her daughter. "Please swallow your repulsion and spend some time at his side. He can hear your prayers."

"He can hear my prayers from here, Mamm. It makes not difference if I am here or there. I cannot bear to see him in such a state with wires poking out of him. Hospitals are filled with harsh lights and harsher people," Hannah countered. "I will not be any good to him there. He knows I am with him in spirit."

Any amount of argument had been futile and eventually Ruth gave up, attending the county hospital with only her two youngest.

"God will not allow him to be taken from us," Ruth assured Hannah one night, attempting to connect with her distraught oldest child.

"God should not have allowed him to have been struck in the first place!" Hannah had yelled back. "God should have been watching out for him. God should have rendered the driver comatose and on life support!"

There was no point in debating the issue. In her mind, Hannah would not rest until she saw the face of the person responsible for the atrocity writhing in shame, guilt and agony.

<u>February</u>

"Ma'am I understand your anger but there we are doing everything we can."

Hannah's blue eyes flashed but she checked her temper.

"Sir, it has been almost three months and you have absolutely no leads regarding the driver of the vehicle which struck my father. Surely you should be exploring other avenues to catch this animal! Doesn't it concern you that this kind of person is driving on your streets where your children walk?"

"Hannah!" Isaac gently placed his hand on her shoulder as she rose from her chair to confront the police detective at the desk. He turned apologetically to the detective.

"Hannah has been under a lot of stress since the accident," Isaac told the man who nodded understandingly.

"Of course, we fully get that and we sympathize," Detective Adams replied. "I have heard that your father is no longer on life support. We are all very happy to hear that."

Hannah felt her hands clench into fists, her nails digging into her palms.

"Yes, praise the Lord for small favors," she answered shortly, her eyes narrowing, ignoring Isaac's fingers which were now increasing pressure on her shoulder. "However, that does not change anything. Is this why nothing has been done to find the monster responsible? Because he is alive? Next time he may not be so lucky if this person is still on the road!"

"Miss Yoder, I assure you that we are doing everything we can but it is very difficult with the circumstances. There were no witnesses, it was a dark road..."

Hannah threw up her hands. She understood. Mark Yoder was not a priority to these people. He would have to be dead or English for them to care. They were just going to say words until she left them alone. Worried she would not be able to contain a barrage of words threatening to escape her lips, she turned to leave without responding. Hannah heard Isaac apologizing for her rudeness once more but Hannah did not wait for her fiancé. Moments later, he was at her side, breathing heavily from chasing her down the crowded street. Under normal circumstances, Hannah would have been unnerved by the throng of people in her midst. It was not like her to visit town, much preferring the quiet way of her community but it had been months and there had been no advancement regarding the driver who had struck her father. Against her mother's pleas, Hannah had taken it upon herself to meet with the detective face-to-face.

"Please, Hannah, Bishop Phillips has been in constant contact with the police. You must not go and bother them."

"If not me, then who?" Hannah had demanded.

"Go see your father! He needs you!" Ruth implored. But the words had fallen upon deaf ears and Ruth had summoned Isaac to accompany her now wayward daughter into town. Isaac had appeared as Hannah was setting off.

"Hannah! That was rude!" He breathed, struggling to keep up with her brisk stride.

"Well perhaps that's what they need, rudeness. Niceties don't seem to be getting us anywhere."

"Hannah, I'm sure they are doing everything they can – "

"It is not enough!" Hannah snapped. Isaac stopped walking, taken aback by her tone. Hannah had never had occasion to speak to him in such a manner. He watched after the woman he was destined to marry and he wondered what had happened to the gentle, even tempered girl he had courted. He understood she was frazzled, not acting rationally but deep down, he hoped that girl was not lost forever.

<u>March</u>

"Hannah, you have not been at worship in several weeks."

The statement was blunt but not filled with accusation. Bishop Phillips simply stared at her, his brown eyes wise with understanding. She shrugged nonchalantly and did not turn from the hens from which she was collecting eggs.

"God knows where I am," she responded flippantly. Bishop Phillips drew closer to her inside the coop, ignoring the squawking of the animals in his midst.

"It is not simply of God knowing where to find you," he told her, gently. "Worship is a place of community, a place where others can shoulder your burden while asking for the Lord's help."

Hannah reeled around to glare at him.

"What does the community know of shouldering my burden?" she asked. "Can they find the animal who ran down my father like a rabid dog in the street? Have they made him pay penance for the harm he has caused my family?"

A warm, fatherly hand reached her shoulder and the Bishop smiled weakly.

"Perhaps not, child, but your suffering is our suffering also. We grow together and we will support one another. That is what makes us strong. You cannot fight this burden alone."

"I am not alone," Hannah retorted. "I have my family. I have Isaac."

But even as she said the words, Hannah tried to remember the last time she had spent more than a few moments with her betrothed. She could not. She shoved the thought from her mind. It did not matter. The only importance was figuring out who had hurt her father. Isaac would have to understand that her priority was with her father.

<u>April</u>

"Hannah! Hannah!"

Miriam and Rachel's footsteps could be heard reverberating through her bedroom well before the door flew open and the twins appeared. Her heart in her throat, Hannah turned away from the window out of which she had been staring for well over an hour, lost in thought.

"What is it? Is it *Daed*? Is he dead?"

Shocked, the girls recoiled at her words, smiles fading from their lips.

"No!" Rachel cried. "Of course not! Why would you say such a thing?"

In truth, Hannah had been waiting for news of the like and had been since the day he had been hospitalized. Her heart began to slow and she forced herself to smile at her sisters.

"I'm sorry. What is it?"

"He's awake! *Daed* is awake!"

Hannah's slowing pulse picked up speed once more. She flung herself into her siblings' arms and the three rejoiced at the news.

"He is? When did this happen? What did the doctors say?" Hannah whipped the questions at them rapid fire. Ruth appeared in the doorway. Her face was gaunt from exhaustion and emotion.

"He will still need some time to recover in the hospital," Ruth answered. "But his ribs are healing as well as his kidneys." Hannah pulled away from the twins and looked at her mother, her face alight with excitement. *Now we will catch you! Daed will identify the driver and it will all be over!*

"Did he say anything?" she pressed. "Can he identify the driver? Or the vehicle? Does he know who hit him?"

Ruth's sky colored eyes clouded over and she regarded her daughter for a moment.

"Hannah, it is not healthy for you to focus so direly on the driver. God will sort out what to do with him. You must instead think of your father and concentrate on good thoughts." Hannah scowled at her mother.

"I am focussed on *Daed*! That is why I want to find out who did this to him! Why am I met with resistance at every turn? You, Isaac, Bishop Phillips. Am I the only one who cares about seeing justice served?"

Ruth pursed her lips together and did not reply. Hannah continued to stare at her mother.

"Well? What did he say? Did he identify the man or not?" she demanded. Ruth sighed heavily.

"No, Hannah. He cannot speak. He had a stroke."

May

Springtime held the promise of new birth for everyone in the community but Hannah. She found herself tending to chores indoor more and more. Isaac had ceased visiting altogether and Hannah found herself in the police station once a week, hounding Detective Adams mercilessly. Where the women in the community would have typically begun to make suggestions for her wedding, offering assistance and chattering cheerfully of their own nuptials, Hannah found herself almost isolated, something she was quite content in discovering. The feeling of helplessness which had overwhelmed her was becoming a suffocating blanket as more time passed and left her no closer to finding the heathen who had hurt her father. She still had not gone to the hospital to see Mark, despite reports from her family that he was faring quite well. He still had not managed to recoup his motor skills and Hannah did not want the face of a crippled man plaguing her already dark thoughts. She would not rest until someone had paid.

June

"You are attending service."

Her voice was flat and left no room for argument. Hannah opened her mouth to speak but caught the anger in her mother's usually gentle eyes and thought better of voicing her thoughts. Grudgingly, she retreated to her room to ready herself for worship.

The family hosting church services was a neighbor and the Yoder family arrived just as Bishop Phillips rose to speak. He fixated his eyes upon Hannah and began to preach of forgiveness. Hannah closed her ears and averted her eyes. *I will forgive when the driver asks for forgiveness. Not one moment before. And even then, I may not.*

July

He came home on a Tuesday and several members of the community were present to welcome Mark. They brought flowers and honey and bombarded him and the family with well wishes. Isaac and his family had driven in also but Hannah only watched the event from her bedroom window, unable to watch her enfeebled father slowly stumble his way up the steps of the veranda. Her eyes filled with tears but whether they were of guilt or pain, she was not sure. As Mark made his way inside with the help of his wife and two youngest daughters, Isaac lifted his eyes toward Hannah's bedroom window. His own eyes were filled with sadness and Hannah quickly ducked back behind the curtains, not willing to look at him. It had been a long while since they had spent time together and she admitted that she missed his company dearly. She often wondered what he was doing and if he thought of her. The look on his face told Hannah that he did long for her as she did him. Swallowing the urge to run downstairs and beg him for forgiveness, Hannah sat on the edge of the bed. She wondered if anything would ever be the same again.

<u>**August**</u>

"Hannah! Hannah!"

Rachel almost knocked Hannah over as she barreled into the barn. Hannah looked up at her quickly.

"What is it?"

"*Daed* said his first clear word!" Hannah felt hope swell in her chest.

"What did he say?" she asked, wiping her hands on her apron and following Rachel out of the building, toward the house.

"He said 'Hannah.' He's asking for you!"

<u>**September**</u>

Progress was swift from that moment onward. Every day, Mark Yoder began to say more. He was required to see a specialist in town to assist him in his walking but Hannah was beginning to see signs of the same, strapping man she had admired her whole life. She found it less painful to be in his presence but she still could not help but feel enraged at his condition. When Hannah did stay at his side, she pressed him for details of the accident. To her relief, he recalled a great deal and Hannah feverishly wrote down the details as Mark remembered, every day adding more to the description. Finally, after three weeks, she had a proper sketch of the vehicle and possibly the driver which she immediately took to the police station. *Now we've got you!* She thought smugly.

<u>**October**</u>

"Are we still to marry?"

The question startled Hannah as she had not heard Isaac at her back. He had been watching her from the porch as she hummed to herself, picking wildflowers. Oddly, the upcoming wedding had been fresh in her mind for the first time in months. Since delivering the description to the police, Hannah had felt as though they were nearing absolution and a giant weight seemed to have been lifted from her shoulders. She stared in surprise at her fiancé.

"I certainly hope so, Isaac. Are you reconsidering?" She felt faint as she waited for him to answer. Slowly, Isaac made his way down the steps and toward his betrothed.

"I feel as though we have become very distant these past months, Hannah. I wondered if you still wished for us to marry." She met the distance between them and offered him her hands.

"Forgive me, Isaac! I have been consumed with worry for my father. Of course I have never thought for a moment that you and I would not be wed." Isaac eagerly accepted her hands and squeezed them gently, smiling with relief.

"I am glad you have finally decided to forgive and move on," he told her. "I knew the sensible woman I know was in there somewhere."

Hannah beamed back at him.

"It will be very easy to move on once this man is caught! I believe the police will finally catch him now!"

The smile died on Isaac's lips as he stared at Hannah. He realized that she was still consumed with the idea of catching the driver. Wisely, he said nothing but a sense of unease filled his stomach. Would this never end?

November

"You must be very excited with the upcoming wedding, Hannah. It has been quite a year for you and your family. It will be a relief to have cause for celebration over bad times, I would say," Bishop Phillips said after service. Hannah smiled widely and nodded, glancing at Isaac. He smiled meekly.

"Yes, we are looking forward to it. A Christmas wedding may seem a bit ostentatious but it is my favorite time of year and Isaac has been kind enough to indulge my whimsy on this matter," Hannah answered happily.

"Well I think it is a wonderful idea. It will only solidify your union with Christ. I am happy to see your father up and about."

"Yes, he is already back into manning the farm as he was prior to the accident."

"Well that is wonderful news, Hannah. It must certainly alleviate your desire to see the perpetrator arrested. It was not good for you to be so fixated on such negative thoughts for so long," the Bishop told her, turning to nod at other members of the congregation.

"No, Bishop, I can focus on other things now. The police are closing in on the animal now that my father has given them somewhere to look. We will have our justice in due time. I must leave it in their hands now." The Bishop looked at Hannah sharply.

"Your father knows who hit him?"

"He gave a very accurate description of the man, yes," Hannah replied. "But as you say, Bishop, it is in God's hands now. I have decided to focus more on my husband-to-be and deal with the criminal when he is found."

Bishop Phillips nodded, his eyes dark.

"Yes, it is in God's hands," he agreed.

<u>December</u>

The police were standing on her porch and Hannah felt her heart leap into her throat.

"Miss Yoder? Is your father home?" the detective asked her, peering over her shoulder. She nodded eagerly and granted them entry. Mark sat in a rocking chair in the front room. He rose to his feet with an agility he did not possess even two weeks prior.

"Please do come in, officers," he told them, cordially. Awkwardly, the detectives ventured into the humble home and stood in the doorway.

"Have you found the man responsible?" Hannah demanded. "Is that why you're here?"

Mark gave her a reproachful look.

"Hannah, where are your manners? Would you like a beverage?" Both men shook their heads and fidgeted nervously.

"Well?" Hannah demanded when there was silence. "Have you news?"

"Hannah!" Mark chided again but the lead detective held up his hand and nodded.

"Yes, Miss Yoder. We have your man. Someone has turned himself in."

Hannah's face went through a variety of changes; hope, shock and then anger.

"He turned himself in?" she almost yelled. "After one year? What kind of monster lets a family suffer for an entire year before confessing his crime?"

"Hannah..."

"Yes, Miss Yoder but frankly, in these situations, it is extremely difficult to find hit and run drivers. We are very lucky that someone did come forward at all," the policeman interjected. "But I do understand your frustration."

"I doubt it," Hannah mumbled. "Where is he?"

"He is in the county lock up. We would like your father to come with us to see if he can be identified in a line up but he had fully confessed to the accident."

"Who is he? A young, drunk English boy?" Hannah asked contemptuously, already envisioning the short haired punk, smoking a marijuana cigarette. Again, an uncomfortable silence ensued. Hannah stared at the men expectantly.

"Who is he?"

Detective Adams cleared his throat.

"It is someone you know," he said evasively. Hannah exchanged concerned looks with her father.

"Who?" she pressed.

"He is your Bishop. Daniel Phillips."

"Hello Hannah."

Hannah felt her legs turn to jelly as she stared at her much-loved Bishop behind the bars of the county jail.

"It is true," she whispered. "How did this happen?"

"I wish I could explain it to you, child but there is nothing I can say which will take away what you and your family have endured over this year."

"Please tell me what happened," she begged, her eyes filled with tears. The Bishop took a breath and told her the story he had relived in his head over and over since the day it had happened.

He had travelled the road hundreds, if not thousands of times before but Bishop Phillips had not slept more than two hours a night in over three weeks. There had been minor unrest in two of the neighboring districts, some petty squabbling which should have resolved itself but somehow a miniscule issue had become a weeks long debate. He was grateful that he was finally able to return home to his district. The car in which he rode had been a gift from a Bishop in one of the districts who had taken pity upon his constant state of commute. Bishop Phillips had to admit that it was more luxurious than his hard riding horse and cart but he also knew that he should not get too attached.

As the headlights lit the way around the road, his heart leapt into his throat. A doe stood frozen in the road, shocked by the onset. In his exhaustion, it took a few seconds for his reaction time to match up with his vision. He slammed on the brakes and veered to the left of the road, barely grazing the tail of the animal but full on impacting something else; a horse drawn cart. The mare whinnied in pain and shock as the Bishop struggled to steady the still moving vehicle. As all was still, Bishop Phillips opened the door to the car and ran toward the now toppled buggy. Inside lay the still body of Mark Yoder, seemingly lifeless. Bishop Phillips stood stock still, unsure of what to do. I must stay and wait for help, he told himself. Then he remembered the two glasses of wine he had consumed with supper. Slowly, he backed up and slipped back into the car, driving away undetected into the black night.

Tears fell from her lids onto her cheeks as she looked at the broken man before her. She thought of how badly she had wanted him to suffer but all she could think of was how much he had already suffered. He must have wanted to ease her agony a thousand times but had been trapped in his own nightmare.

"I understand that you must loathe me, Hannah. You have every right to feel as such," Bishop Phillips told her, his voice cracking. Gently, Hannah reached between the bars and offered the Bishop her hands. He grabbed them instantly and looked at her pleadingly.

"I forgive you," she said simply.

<u>Christmas</u>

"Oh, Hannah you look beautiful," Ruth told her daughter, embracing her warmly. "I have been looking forward to this for so long!"

Hannah laughed.

"Yes, me too *Mammi*," she joked and lovingly returned her mother's caress. She looked at herself in the mirror one last time. She vowed to her reflection that with this new start she would forsake all anger and rely on God to give her strength in the worst of times. She knew how fortunate she was that Isaac had been strong enough to stand by her during such a trying time and she would never forget it. She turned and looked at her mother and sisters.

"Are you ready?" Miriam asked, hopping back and forth from one foot to another. Hannah looked around and suddenly her stomach dropped.

"Where is *Daed*?" she asked, feeling a familiar sense of panic seize her. The curtain was quickly drawn and Mark strolled in, his gait strong and perfect.

"I am here, *liebchen*. Do you think I would miss giving away my oldest daughter?" he answered. His voice was slightly slower than it had been but his words were perfectly pronounced. There was no sign of the stroke he had suffered. Hannah exhaled. Everything was right again.